CRIME WAVE

Published in the United States by Random House Children's Books, a division of Penguin
Random House LLC, 1745 Broadway, New York, NY 10019, and in Canada by Penguin
Random House Canada Limited, Toronto. Random House and the colophon are registered
trademarks of Penguin Random House LLC.

rhcbooks.com

ISBN 978-0-593-90380-3 (trade)

Printed in the United States of America

10 9 8 7 6 5 4 3 2 1

CRIME WAVE

By Matthew J. Gilbert

Based on the screenplays
"Raph vs. Water" and "Donnie Goes Deep" by Matthew Bass,
"Mikey Takes Charge" and "The Pear" by Alex Hanson,
"Splinter and April Fight a Goldfish" by Haley Mancini,
and "Leonardo Saddles Up" by Elise Roncace

Random House New York

CHAPTER 1
APRIL

April O'Neil here, with a story for you. It's bold. It's important. It's . . . all in squeaking noises.

How is anyone gonna understand this?

I interviewed Splinter for a class assignment. I asked him what it was like to brave the big storm down here, in the sewers, where there's no escaping the flood.

He spoke for, like, six hours straight about the event. Sounds like a good interview and an even better grade, right? Well, it would be, but it's all in *squeaks*.

I know he speaks English. He does it all the time!

The Turtles told me he's not squeaking but speaking a bizarre insect language no human being can understand called "vermin." He learned it to communicate with his mutant girlfriend, Scumbug.

I showed the Turtles my Splinter footage, hoping they could help in some way. "Six hours of video, and it's all *that.* He just squeaks. What am I going to do?"

"Vermin or not, Dad can't tell a story," Raph said matter-of-factly. "And besides, the storm was dumb. Nothing even happened."

Donnie scowled at that. "The whole city flooded! Everyone lost power!"

"Whatever! You gotta give the people what they want! Add in a fight, put some monsters in there, maybe a heist or something. Have Donnie get eaten!"

"But none of that happened!" I said.

As a serious journalist, I would *never* make anything up. I have a sacred bond with my viewers. They trust me to deliver the truth about really occurred, not some sensationalized fanfic I made up for clicks.

"You want a good grade on this thing, right?" Raph asked.

He had a point. No one was going to listen to a reporter with an F in journalism class.

Raph started typing. "Let me tell you a story. . . ."

RAPHAEL

The storm was raging.

But I was about to rage even harder.

Everywhere I went, it was like I couldn't get away from the water. Topside, the rain made everyone walk slower, which made it impossible to not get completely soaking wet. The taxi cabs were driving through these puddles and splashing mini tidal waves on every street corner.

Down below, the sewers were even worse.

The ceiling was leaking. The walls were dripping. And a wave of unexpected guests had rolled in.

The Mutanimals were staying with us, and as much as I liked those guys, they were really getting on my nerves.

Like the newest Mutanimal, Pigeon Pete. He shed feathers everywhere, and when he wasn't cooing, he was pooing. Thankfully, Splinter put Leo in charge of babysitting the birdbrain. "Pete! Pete, wait!" Leo yelled, racing after him, hoping to herd him into the bathroom before it was too late.

It was always *too late.*

Wingnut, the bat girl, would drive anyone batty with her constant talking. Anyone except Donnie. When the two of them got together, talking about anime nonstop, it was like a *nerd-off.*

Right now, they were supposed to be working on the lair's electrical grid to make sure we didn't lose power during the storm. But instead, they were getting all excited about *Avatar: The Last Airbender.* Wingnut was so psyched, she accidentally smacked me with her wing.

Talk about a slap in the face!

I hit the fridge, thinking a little snack would cheer me up. *I thought wrong.*

I found Michelangelo and Genghis Frog in the kitchen, arguing about who had eaten what. There was no more food and no more soda. Unless you wanted to drink the two-liter that Genghis barfed up.

I wasn't that thirsty.

I tried to get a moment by myself to think, when I tripped over something and face-planted into a puddle.

And to my surprise, the puddle had a face!

It was Ray Fillet, the manta ray. "Ray Fillet!" he sang with a smile—completely clueless that he'd made me fall over.

"Good morning!" I heard Dad say. "It's another beautiful day in our sewer home."

I exploded. "NO, IT'S NOT! THIS SUCKS! We've been trapped down here because of this stupid storm. Everything's soaked, the power's going out, they canceled school, they canceled wrestling practice. The Octagon, where I kickbox, is flooded. Not to mention we're stuck down here with the Mutanimals!"

Dad tried to put a positive spin on the situation. "They are sheltering in place with us during the storm. It's quite nice to have the company—"

"Okay, but Pigeon Pete is using my bed as a bathroom."

"Are you doing your meditations? Remember what we talked about? Chopping wood?"

I pointed to the stacks of chopped wood in the corner. The axe was still buried in the floor where I left it. "I chopped all the wood! Everyone's always in my face! I can't hear myself think!"

Sensing my anger, Dad looked past me and saw the chaos that we had been living in. He clocked Leo chasing Pete from bedroom to bedroom, and Genghis trying to wrap Mikey up with his slimy frog tongue.

"We are all on edge," Dad admitted.

Instead of yelling, he focused his attention on me, making me hug a pillow.

He called it "the meditation pillow."

"Breathe in . . . breathe out," Dad instructed.

After a few breaths, I finally calmed down. My muscles loosened up, and I slowly felt like I could breathe again.

Until a jackhammer started up somewhere on the surface. It vibrated the sewers and made my head feel like it was rolling around inside a washing machine on the highest speed. The world looked like it was shaking.

I had a meltdown.

My temper exploded, and I tore the meditation pillow in half. I toppled the bookcase. I flipped a few tables. The storm was outside, but in here, Hurricane Raphael had made landfall.

And I laid a path of destruction.

When there were no more things to destroy, I stopped to catch my breath.

Leo approached and tried to calm me down. *Big mistake.*

"It's just a construction crew, probably," he explained. "Just shoring up the river walls, prevent more flooding. It's a good thing."

I tackled Leo and dragged him through the puddles in our living room.

"Use your words!" Leo said, trying to fight me off.

"I'm done talking!" I told him, using him like a wrecking ball.

Our fight inspired more fights to break out across the lair. I guess everyone had finally had enough. It was a free-for-all!

Dad spoke up and got everyone under control. I don't remember every little squeak, but I'll do my best to translate for you. He basically said, "I changed my mind! Raphael is right. You all need to get out of here!"

His command stopped every fight mid-punch. We all listened closely, even if we couldn't believe our ears.

"You want us to go outside?" Mikey asked.

"It's raining!" Donnie said.

"You are Turtles!" Dad scolded us. "A little water will do you good. Stretch your legs, find a little purpose."

He turned to each of us, giving his instructions. . . .

"Leonardo, take Pete out for some air!

"Michelangelo, go to the market with Genghis and replenish our supplies!

"Donatello, you and Wingnut fix the power so I can watch my shows!

"And, Raphael . . . find that jackhammer and tell it to be quiet."

I cracked my knuckles, grateful for the solo mission. "With pleasure."

As I was about to leave, he dropped this on me: "And take Ray Fillet and Scumbug with you."

"What?! No way! This is a one-person job," I protested.

Dad gave me a look that said *this is not a discussion*.

"You need them, as they need you," he said.

Ray and Scumbug gingerly walked over, clearly way more excited to be with me than I was to be with them.

"OKAY, FILLET!" Ray Fillet said.

And Scumbug agreed . . . in *vermin,* of course.

Her squeaks sounded happy.

As more water came leaking in, we all made our way out of the lair to go our separate ways.

Everyone else headed topside. But I led Ray and Scumbug deeper into the sewer tunnels.

And even deeper into troubled waters.

The farther we walked, the louder the jackhammering got. I could barely hear myself think.

Ray Fillet was living his best life, though. "Ray Fillet!" he shouted, happily splashing around in the water.

"Man, you are loving this water, Ray," I said, kinda grossed out. "You know that's like poop water, right? I wouldn't swim in it, if I were you."

Ray didn't care. He dove headfirst, sliding around with his fins. To be honest, it kinda made me queasy.

Scumbug tried joining in on the conversation, but it was all sqeaks to me.

"Still no idea what you're saying, Scumbug," I told her.

Just then, the jackhammering sound returned. The

vibrations were so strong, they shook some gunk and debris loose from above. It nearly knocked me off my feet!

"All right, this sounds like the place," I yelled over the noise. "Gonna find this thing, gonna shut it up."

I steadied myself and followed the sound to a wide-open space where all the sewer tunnels converged.

It was like walking into a huge warehouse . . . or actually, *wading* into one. The rain had made the sewer waters rise to our waists, so we had to swim if we wanted to go any farther.

Toward the giant machines at the far end of the room.

They were construction vehicles, but only one was moving. It was the same one making that awful noise and rumbling the tunnels like an earthquake.

To my surprise, this was no jackhammer. It was a drill about to break through the surface!

"Hey, can you turn that thing off?" I yelled, but the driver inside couldn't hear me over the noise.

I looked to the others for help. Ray was off swimming again, and Scumbug just stared back at me, confused, twiddling her wings.

"Ah, forget it," I said, taking matters into my own hands. I spotted a heavy rock under the water and lobbed it at the drill like a football. *CRAAASH!* It bounced off the driver's side door with a bang—loud enough to make him stop drilling.

I expected him to come out, ready to argue. That was how construction workers normally were in this city. But not this guy. He started crying! As he spoke through his tears, I was able to make out that his name was Stephen.

"What are you doing down here?" I asked him.

"I'm digging a hole up to the surface." He sniffled. "That's what you wanted, wasn't it?"

Huh? Stephen must have had me confused with someone else.

Just then, I heard a stirring in the water behind me. I turned, expecting to see Ray swim up, but there was no one.

No Ray Fillet. And now, mysteriously, no Scumbug.

All that was left were ripples in the water.

"They're back!" Stephen panicked, hiding in fear. Like he knew what was really going on.

That made one of us.

"Who's *they*?" I asked.

Suddenly, something strong pulled me under the water. It felt like seaweed, but I knew better. Seaweed was found on beaches, not in this part of the sewer. It also couldn't crush you like a pro wrestler putting you in a serious headlock.

This was something else. Something powerful. This was *them*.

And whoever—or whatever—they were, they had a tentacle wrapped around my leg.

A freaking *tentacle*!

It took all of me not to freak out under the water. I held my breath and tried to stay calm. I wouldn't need the meditation pillow this time.

This time, I'd go with something a little sharper: my sai.

I unhooked them from my belt and went to town on the tentacle until this *thing* finally released its slimy grip on me. I swam away, spotting another set of tentacles pulling someone else down.

I'd know that face anywhere—it was Scumbug! *They* were pulling her deeper into the dirty depths, too! The air bubbles fluttered out of her mandibles like *help meeee!*

I lunged forward and whacked the tentacles away, freeing her to swim up to safety with me. *SPLAAAASH!*

We came up for air, scrambling onto a pile of floating garbage. Scumbug started squeaking in vermin right away, so I knew she could breathe A-OK.

I spotted Stephen, still cowering. "What were those things?!"

"Is that, like, a trick question?" he asked, suddenly confused. "You're not with them?"

I wanted to yell, *Them WHO?!*

But there was no need.

They finally rose from the water—four pink, blobby creatures with tentacles coming out of their heads. I didn't know what they were exactly.

All I knew was that they were the weirdest-looking mutants I'd ever seen.

Have you ever seen a sea anemone before? They're these underwater creatures that look like they have a gooey cheerleader pom-pom for a head. That was what these things reminded me of—sea anemones.

More like sea *enemies*.

These guys may have looked silly, but they were not giving off a friendly vibe. They surrounded me and started . . . quoting TV commercials?

"Call before you dig!"

"Limited time offer! Sign up today!"

"Talk to your doctor about harmful side effects!"

I gripped my sai tight, ready to strike. I wasn't going to let their weird TV quote-a-thon throw me off my ninja game. "I don't want to hurt you guys," I said, before quickly changing my mind. "Actually, I kinda do."

I burst into action, charging the sea enemy closest to me. He tried swatting me away with his tentacles, but it was no use—I was too fast for his slimy attacks. With one swipe of my sai, I sliced through the air . . . and

straight through his tentacle!

It fell off his body and into the water with a *splash!*

Gross, right? That's nothing.

I watched in complete disgust as the tentacle *grew back* right before my eyes! Nature can be cool, but it makes me want to barf sometimes.

Scumbug and I had that in common, I guess, because it looked like she was about to hurl. The other sea enemies ganged up on me, and there were one too many tentacles for me to fight off. A few of their slimy arms caught my wrists and started to squeeze me into submission. They lifted me into the air, turning me into a floating punching bag. *THWACK THWACK THWACK!*

After a few dozen tentacle punches, I couldn't see straight, let alone grip my sai. I couldn't get away. I needed backup, bad.

I looked down at Scumbug. "Are you gonna help or not?"

I didn't speak vermin, and I was a little dazed from all the hits, but her squeaking sounded almost . . . *confident.* Like she was trying to say, *Don't worry, help is on the way, Raph.*

And by *help*, she meant bug barf.

Scumbug vomited up a stream of roach acid powerful enough to make the sea enemies back off. They didn't know what had hit them. All they could do was quote commercials about cleaning products and doctor visits.

"Disinfect your home!"

"See your doctor immediately!"

The tentacle-heads were so grossed out, they loosened their grip on me. I used the distraction to slip out and slam one of them into the wall.

Bits of concrete started raining down. I didn't think I'd thrown him that hard, but maybe I didn't know my own strength!

Or maybe the drill was back on.

That awful, earthshaking sound returned, echoing off the sewer walls. I looked at the drill machine, seeing Stephen inside at the controls again, this time under the watchful eye of a sea enemy standing over his shoulder. A mix of debris and rainwater sprayed over us as the drill kicked into high gear, destroying a bunch of water pipes in the process.

"If he keeps digging, this whole place is gonna flood,"

I said to Scumbug, concerned. "We gotta stop him."

SPLASH! I waded toward the drill as fast as I could. The water was slowing me down.

I tried yelling to Stephen over the drilling, but there was no way he could hear me over the sound of breaking rock ... and the loud *crash* that happened right after.

The ceiling caved in on top of us, and floodwater rushed over my head.

The sewers were underwater.

And we were in deep, *deep* trouble.

Turtles can do a lot of cool things, but we can't breathe underwater.

I needed air, but the power of the flood kept pushing me farther down. My arms were getting heavier, and so were my eyelids. It was dark down here, and hard to see a path back to the surface.

The longer I stayed under, the more my eyes played tricks on me. I watched a shadow swimming through a cloud of inky dirt and air bubbles. It wasn't blobby enough to be a sea enemy. Was that a giant log drifting toward me? Or a bunch of trash?

Or could it be . . .

"RAY FILLET!"

Before I knew it, I was moving through the water, fast. Like I was riding on top of a geyser shooting straight up. We finally broke through the surface.

I took a deep breath and opened my eyes—just in time to see Ray Fillet about to give me mouth-to-mouth resuscitation.

"Thank you," I gargled, stopping Ray before his mouth got any closer to mine.

I sat up, snapping out of it. We were floating on a large chunk of concrete that was sitting on top of the rushing waters like a raft.

Ray dove down and came back up with Scumbug. He gently put her next to me. She was alive and breathing— which meant she was squeaking.

I got a good look at the damage around us. Flood-water and rain from the topside mixed together in a mighty storm surge, rushing through the giant hole in the ceiling. The sewers were filling up faster than one of

Mikey's cereal bowls.

It kinda felt like we were lost at sea. Just the three of us. If we were going to survive this, we needed each other. Just like Dad said.

I turned to Ray and Scumbug. "Look, I know I was angry and yelled at you guys . . . but I think my anger stopped us from working together, like a team. Like me and my brothers," I said, doing my best to stay calm. Like Dad taught me. "We can do this."

We stealthily swam back together. We could see the drill machine situated on a patch of dry land up ahead, just above the rushing water. Stephen was still at the controls, while the sea enemies stood guard.

We used the water to our advantage, blowing bubbles to catch the curiosity of one of the blobby mutants . . . who got a little too close so she could take a look.

FWOOM! Ray popped out of the water and pulled her down with him.

Another sea enemy stopped his patrol when he heard

a strange squeaking coming from somewhere near the drill. He looked around but didn't see anything odd . . . until he looked straight up.

That was when Scumbug leapt down from above, tackling him without a squeak.

The third sea enemy was all mine. Using ninja silence, I snuck up behind him and used his own tentacles to tie him up.

Three enemies down, one more to go.

The last sea enemy left Stephen alone to see what all the commotion was. He was confused, seeing only me standing there. "In an accident?" the sea enemy asked, quoting yet another commercial.

"That's right!" I sarcastically replied. "Your friends were in an accident! And you're about to be in one, too."

Before I could surprise him with a punch, Stephen surprised me. . . .

By driving his drill machine straight into the sea enemy! *WHAM!*

I guess he was tired of being bossed around by the blobs.

We watched the blobby mutant launch through the

air, hit the water, and sink out of view.

"Nice job," I told Stephen. "Now tell me why they were making you do this?"

Stephen spilled his guts. It was clear he was only drilling because the sea enemies had bullied him into it. He seemed just as panicked by the flooding as we were.

"They wanted me to drill up into the city," Stephen confessed. "But they said something about the seawall. They wanted to take it down, too. Which would be bad."

"How bad?"

"The entire city would have flooded."

"Oh, that's bad."

Something occurred to me. "Hey, how did you even figure out what they were telling you to do?" I asked, curious if Steve understood their constant quotes. Maybe he watched a lot of TV, too?

"They didn't tell me anything," he answered. "It was the *others*. They gave me this."

Others?! There are more *of those things?!*

Stephen showed me things I wasn't supposed to see: A map with sites circled on it. Along with a pamphlet for the Natural History Museum.

The flood was only the beginning. Whoever was behind this had much bigger plans.

Suddenly I could hear voices coming from the other side of the drill machine. Someone else was in the sewers with us!

Ray and Scumbug hid with Stephen, while I carefully snuck a peek at something coming out of the water. . . .

It was the sea enemies. . . .

Followed by three river mutants I'd never seen before: an electric eel, a scary-looking seahorse, and a tiny goldfish who acted like the *big boss*.

I couldn't hear them, but I managed to read their lips. . . .

"Proceed with the plan. . . ."

"If the Turtles interfere, deal with them. . . ."

"East River Three . . ."

I'd heard . . . I mean, *read* . . . enough. This East River Three was bad news, and they were about to make this storm a whole lot worse.

CHAPTER 2
MICHELANGELO

Ah, another night in the life of a Ninja Turtle....

But this wasn't just a regular night. This was one of those rainy nights you see on the news, when reporters get knocked down in the storm—and you feel bad for them, but you still laugh when someone makes a GIF of it, you know?

Well, I wasn't laughing.

I was too busy getting rainwater in my mouth—just from opening the sewer cover to go up to the surface!

Genghis didn't seem to mind the weather. Or if he did, he didn't say. He was a frog of few words, which meant I did most of the talking whenever we went out.

"I wasn't even doing anything. I just pointed out that you ate all the food! Now I'm the one who has to go on a supply run in the middle of a storm!"

"If you don't like being the errand boy, do something about it," Genghis suggested. "Take charge."

He had a point, even though it wasn't really my style. I was more of a *take a break* kinda guy, not a *take charge* kinda guy.

"Eh, it's fine," I said, shaking off the negativity. "I actually don't mind going out. But, like, I want it to be *my* choice. Come on . . . some fresh air, a little hydration, the feel of the wind on your face! What's not to love?"

Suddenly the wind picked up a hot dog cart and launched it through the air.

Genghis and I gave each other a *that was close* look.

I glanced up at the sky just as more thunder cracked above us. We needed to get out of the elements. And fast.

The bright lights of our friendly neighborhood bodega were shining up ahead—like a lighthouse in the storm. "Come on, cuz, let's get some snacks!"

There is no better shelter from the storm than your neighborhood bodega.

Think about it: If the power goes out, or the world ends, you're covered! You're inside the cutest little grocery store with all the potato chips and candy bars you're ever gonna need! And you've got the kindest hosts in the entire city there—in our case, Ms. Khatri and her adorably grumpy cat, Mr. Whiskers.

This place was our little piece of paradise.

Genghis and I rushed in, getting out of the rain.

"Ms. Khatri!" I beamed. "I wasn't sure you were gonna be open with the storm and all!"

I expected her usual cheery hello . . . but that was not the welcome we got. We walked up to the counter to find her nervously standing there with a mysterious stranger.

A mean-looking girl wearing lots of purple.

"Yes, we are open," Ms. Khatri said awkwardly. "Are you here for groceries?"

"Yes, we are!" I replied, pointing to my croaking cousin. "This is Genghis Frog!"

Genghis did his usual *CROOOOOAK*.

"Hey, I haven't seen you before," I said to the new girl. "Do you work here?"

"Yeah, just started," she said. "I'm . . . uhhh . . . Angela."

Awkward to think about your own name, but, hey, she's probably a little nervous around mutants, I thought.

"Well, nice to meet you, Angela!" I said. "We're gonna grab some supplies, if that's cool. C'mon, Genghis."

I found a tote and hit the aisles to begin our shopping. I thought Genghis was right behind me, but he got distracted chasing Mr. Whiskers around.

As I entered the first aisle, I was shocked to see the state of the store. There were damaged shelves and perfectly good junk food scattered on the floor. "This place is a mess! Did it get crazy in here because of the storm?" I wondered out loud. "Are people hoarding?"

I headed to the back of the store and found two other people, who were also *unusually tense.*

Two girls. One of them was wearing purple and had a

cane. She seemed a little weirded out to see me.

"How's it going!" I said to her. "You look freaked out, but don't be! Even though I'm a famous mutant, I'm still a normal guy doing some shopping, just like you."

Off to the side, I noticed more shoppers. One of them was a muscular giant *also wearing purple.* The other was a sweet old man I recognized from around the neighborhood. He usually gave me a polite nod, but not this time.

I shrugged it off and kept shopping. I noticed that strange people were now *closing in on me.* Now that they were closer, they seemed kinda dangerous....

Because they were.

I realized it too late. They weren't simply wearing purple; they were Purple Dragons—the street gang!

"Wait, are you guys robbing this place?" I asked, putting the pieces together.

"Finally!" Ms. Khatri sighed.

So that was why everyone was acting so weird! They were hostages.

"All right, freaks, get down on the ground unless you want people to get hurt!" the leader of the Purple Dragons demanded.

I knew who these jerks were. Even though we'd never met, I'd heard all about them from a very reliable source. "You're *Angel*! And the big guy, he's Hun; he's obsessed with chickens. Raph told me about you guys."

Angel was clearly done talking. "Look, me and my Dragons are gonna walk out of here with our haul. And you and that—whatever that thing is," she said, motioning to Genghis, "you're gonna let us. Or the old lady gets it."

The last thing I wanted was for anyone to get hurt, so I lowered my nunchucks. "Fine by me. Just go."

"The axe, too," Angel demanded, talking about Genghis's axe.

Genghis wasn't touching his axe. I don't even think he was aware he was standing two feet away from a robbery in progress. He was just trying to get close to Mr. Whiskers.

A little too close. He'd cornered the little kitty high up on a shelf. The Mutanimals were sweet, but I had to remind myself, they were still wild animals!

"Put the axe down!" Hun shouted.

Genghis ignored him, licking his lips like he was looking at a snack. A furry feline snack.

Without warning, his long frog tongue suddenly *shot out* of his mouth, gobbling up Mr. Whiskers in one swift gulp!

"No!" I yelled. "Mr. Whiskers isn't food!"

Before I could save the cat, Hun was already on it, charging at Genghis. Raph had told me this guy was a serious animal lover, and he was not kidding. He looked like he was going to punch the bodega cat right out of Genghis's gut if he didn't cough him up. "Spit him out! He's just an innocent kitty!"

Things were uneasy in this standoff, but they were about to get a whole lot shakier!

A shock wave rattled the floor underneath us, followed by a weird, high-pitched noise. The kinda thing that would make the hairs on the back of my neck stand up . . . *if, you know, I had any hair!*

We all stopped to look at one another—each of us unsure of what was going on outside the bodega walls.

"Was that an earthquake?" I asked.

"New York doesn't get earthquakes," Angel replied.

She looked to Hun, ready to make her getaway—but Hun wasn't done. Not until Mr. Whiskers was free to roam the store again. He'd climbed up to Genghis and forced him to cough up the cat.

RAIIIRRRR! Mr. Whiskers came flying out of Genghis's mouth, knocking Cane Girl and Angel against the wall like a furry, wet cannonball.

This was my chance—they were distracted. I could leap into action and save my neighborhood bodega. I was about to take a crack at the Dragons . . .

. . . when the ground suddenly cracked below my feet!

RUMMMBLE! The walls shook violently, the lights flickered, and the floor collapsed into a huge sinkhole that swallowed me up.

Now I knew how Mr. Whiskers felt.

"AAAAII!" Ms. Khatri screamed, falling in right behind me.

I caught her in a split second, holding on to her hand as water started to fill the sinkhole below us.

I looked up at what I was gripping with my other hand—it was a busted pipe sticking out from the wreckage in the store. It was bent but still strong enough to hold us. "Okay, this is fine, it's gonna be fine." I tried to put on a brave face for her. "Things can't get any worse than this, right?"

On cue, the shriek sliced through the air again. That wasn't from the storm. It sounded like a monster screeching somewhere in the night.

Ms. Khatri was beginning to panic. And her hand was starting to *slip.*

I looked past her, seeing bubbles in the water.

"There's something down there!" she screamed.

She was right. Something big was slithering around underneath us . . . and the water was lifting it toward us.

Thankfully, the old man from before leaned over the sinkhole, reaching his hand out for Ms. Khatri's.

She looked at the old man with love in her eyes. "Oh, Harold . . ."

I felt like I was suddenly in the cutest rom-com ever, but now was hardly the time. "Lovin' this vibe, but we gotta move," I told them.

The old man lifted Ms. Khatri out of the sinkhole. I flipped up, landing next to them.

All eyes—shoppers', Dragons', and animals'—were on me. "Okay, I don't want to freak anyone out, but there's possibly a tiny chance there's a monster in here with us."

No response. They all just kept staring.

"Why's everyone looking at me? I'm not in charge. I just came to get groceries," I said.

"You're supposed to be some kind of hero," Angel replied. "Figure it out!"

More dirty water spilled out from the sinkhole onto the floor. It was rising quicker and quicker—first around our ankles. Soon it'd be around our waists. This whole store was filling up like a fish tank.

There was no way out.

And we were officially trapped inside with *whatever* was swimming around down there.

"Climb the shelves!" I shouted.

Everyone followed my lead, scaling the walls to reach

the highest—and driest—areas left in the store. . . .

The shelves.

Ms. Khatri and her new (but still *old*) boyfriend shared a shelf. The rest of the shelves were quickly claimed by the others—hostages and Dragons alike. We all found a place, except for the giant Hun, who was obviously way too big and heavy to safely fit anywhere.

"Get on the counter!" Angel yelled at him.

Hun took one look at the counter and the water rising around it. The thing in the water—whatever it was—swam up from the sinkhole and circled the counter like a shark circles a boat.

"That's not fair!" he observed.

Fair? No. But strong enough to hold a muscley dude without crumbling? Probably.

Seeing no other option, Hun reluctantly joined the other heavy lunkhead on the counter, Genghis.

We were all now in the clear and out of the water. . . .

Away from danger . . .

Away from the freaky swimming *thing* . . .

Until Genghis decided to wild out. Again.

He dove in, hoping for another shot at Mr. Whiskers!

"Get out of the water," I pleaded. But it was no use! All he could see was the snack that got away.

He didn't see the *giant snake thing* swimming up closer.

What happened next was truly shocking: the thing shrieked and let out a burst of electricity that lit everything up . . . including Genghis!

The zap threw him back onto the countertop—there was literal smoke coming off his body, I kid you not!

"Maybe . . . I don't want the cat . . . that bad," Genghis said, finally giving up.

Genghis had been *electrocuted*. I had never seen water do that to a frog.

The water splashed and crackled with energy bolts like something was charging it up.

It had to be *THE THING*!

It was fine, still swimming . . . but also sparking. I knew for sure that sharks didn't shock.

We were dealing with an *electric eel*!

This took the danger to a whole new level. "The water's electrified! Stay out of the water!" I warned.

I looked around again to see where the thing was . . . right when it suddenly popped up, hissing in my face!

I could see now that this was no ordinary electric eel. It stood tall, thanks to its mutated legs. And thanks to its bulging, mutant arms . . . it could also tackle.

The mutant eel lunged at me, and we both went crashing through the wall.

I missed falling into the electrified water. Somehow.

Maybe it was luck—if you can call being tackled by a giant mutant eel *lucky*.

I landed on a table in one of those Employees Only back rooms. It was also flooding back here.

The eel hissed again. Nothing between me and its fangs but a crate.

"Man, you are really terrifying!" I said, almost as a compliment. "Can we talk about this? Do you even talk?"

She did.

"Goldfin said you'd try to stop us, but I won't let you," the eel revealed.

I had so many questions. "Who's Goldfin? And stop you from doing what?"

"From getting to the museum!"

"Why would I care if you go to the museum? Museums are great! Have you seen Van Gogh's work in person? It's, like, life-changing," I told her.

"No, I haven't been, but now I'd really like to see it . . . ," she said, accidentally lightening up for a sec, like we weren't in the middle of a fight.

She snapped back into beast mode. "Hey, stop mocking me!"

There were those bulging arms again—she threw me across the room!

"You're trying to confuse me!" she hissed. "The other Turtle tried to stop us from tunneling into the museum, and now you're here in my way? You expect me to believe that you're just here to get groceries?"

My eyes went wide. *Museum?! Other Turtle?! What is she talking about?!*

"We're gonna fight!" she said.

"I don't want to fight! I don't even know your name!" I said nervously.

Again, she softened up for a moment. "Oh, it's Lee."

I tried not to laugh. "Lee the Eel? That's just *eel* spelled backward! Oh dang, I guess I am mocking you now."

That made her *really* angry. She lunged at me with her jaws open. *CHOMP!*

I dodged as best I could and looked for a way out of this. I could see the hole we made in the wall . . . and the flooded store on the other side.

I didn't want to be eel food, so I decided to jump for it!

Swinging my nunchucks, I leapt forward, whapping Lee with a quick hit. Then I used her head as a stepping stone to launch myself farther out. . . .

And *boom,* it wasn't quite a hole in one . . . but one in the hole!

"You hit me!" Lee said, almost insulted that I'd fought back.

"You're trying to eat me!" I explained.

"No! I'd probably just bite you real hard, and then, like, shock you."

"Oh, well, that's okay," I joked. "I'll just stay still."

"Really?" she said, becoming friendly again. "Wait. WAIT—ARE YOU MAKING FUN OF ME?!"

I was.

Lee tail-whipped me—which was just the thrust I

needed to make it back to the shelves in the store! I went flying in!

Lee ran through the water, chasing me back through the hole. I was prepared to continue our fight in the bodega, but I didn't need to.

Because the bodega decided to fight back!

The hostages and the Dragons put their differences aside to work together. They threw whatever was left on their shelves at her—mostly cans. They were just the reinforcements I needed to make Lee back off. After a few hard hits, she retreated underwater.

But she didn't go too far.

I could see a dark shape patiently circling, zapping the water with volts of crackling electricity.

Lee the electric eel would be back in a flash!

I usually loved being the center of attention. Not tonight.

BZZRT! BZZRT! The zaps in the water lit up the store enough for me to see everyone's eyes on me again. It kinda reminded me of being onstage with my improv group. Except these people didn't want to laugh, they wanted to live.

Talk about pressure!

"You're all giving me that look again," I said. "I don't know what to do, okay? I'm just trying not to get eaten!"

Suddenly Lee made her move—bursting up from the water! I stumbled back, barely catching my balance on the coolers in the back of the store.

This was too close for Cane Girl's comfort. She leapt off her shelf to get away from Lee and me, grabbing hold of a ceiling beam to swing over.

Bad idea.

"You're too heavy!" Angel observed.

She accidentally brought a section of the ceiling down. Chunks of the roof fell, knocking into the shelf shared by Ms. Khatri and Harold. Their ledge started to buckle, lowering the cute old couple dangerously close to the electrified waters.

I was too far back in the store to save them, and there was no easy path for me to get near them. They didn't have long. Another few seconds and they'd be electrocuted worse than Genghis.

"Someone help them!" I pleaded. "Anyone?!"

The others all just stared back at me—afraid. They didn't know what to do. Neither did I.

Whenever I felt that way, it usually meant there was only one thing left to do....

Don't think, I told myself. *Improvise.*

Just like in improv class, it all came to me in the moment.

I had my audience: *Lee the Eel.*

I had a prop: *the wires hanging down from the broken ceiling.*

And, yes, I had a scene partner: *Mr. Whiskers.*

I could see the grumpy feline prancing around in the background, trying desperately to get away from Genghis. *Classic Mr. Whiskers,* I thought. Time to put my impromptu plan into action.

"Hey, I'm sorry about before," I said to Lee, sounding sincere. "It wasn't cool for me to laugh at your name."

This caught Lee off guard. "Wait, are we being serious for a moment? Because that actually means a lot to me."

"Your super-ridiculous, dumb, backward name!"

I said, revealing how I really felt.

This sent Lee into a shocking rage. *HIIISSS!* She took a flying leap, lunging straight at me....

Just like before, her weird, slimy head was the perfect stepping stone!

Time seemed to stand still in that cool, ninja slow-mo way. I wish I could have watched it and rewound it, because there was a lot of awesome stuff happening at once, all in midair. Here's how it went down....

Just as Ms. Khatri and Harold's shelf collapsed ...

Mr. Whiskers launched through the air to get away from Genghis ...

I sprang forward, leapfrogging off Lee's head again ...

Somehow spinning, catching the cat ...

Making Lee leap after me ...

And go totally airborne ...

Which meant she was finally out of the water ...

Just as Ms. Khatri and Harold dropped down with a *SPLASH!*

"We're alive!" Ms. Khatri gasped in disbelief. "I don't understand."

"He got the monster out of the water," Harold

realized. "It's de-electrified."

The others wasted no time dropping down from their shelves and safely swimming toward the exit.

The best part: Lee caught the whole thing. You see, she actually had the best seat in the house . . . since she was tangled in the wires on the ceiling, trapped in midair, like a bug in a spiderweb. Totally powerless.

Talk about being a *captive* audience!

Aaaaand, scene! Hold your applause. Or don't. Okay, give me a standing ovation! YES!

I landed shell-first into the water, careful to keep Mr. Whiskers held high above it, nice and dry.

"You saved the cat," Hun said, relieved.

"You saved us all." Ms. Khatri smiled.

I couldn't contain my excitement. "I totally did it! Improv skills for the win!"

We eventually got the front doors open, and everyone made it out alive. Wet and smelly, but alive.

Ms. Khatri and Harold thanked me. The other

hostages thanked me. Even the Dragons thanked me.

The only one I didn't hear a peep from was Lee the Eel . . .

Since she had suddenly vanished during our goodbyes.

"That can't be good," I said, looking at Genghis. "We gotta warn the others."

CHAPTER 3
APRIL

I'm sure you're wondering where I was during this whole freak storm, am I right?

Well, I was actually *on the scene*—which is reporter-speak for . . . standing out in the rain. No umbrella, no camera crew. Just me, recording on my phone.

I can admit, it was not my finest hour of news.

"It's been raining nonstop for four days," I said, trying to spice up my intro. "This may be the storm of the cen— UGH."

A gust of rain hit me. "Okay, you know what? Storm of the century or not, I'm done reporting the weather."

"It's raining!" this random old lady informed me.

Like I wasn't standing in the same exact rain she was.

"Yeah, I know," I said. "What are you even doing outside? It's not safe! Go home!"

Just then, I heard a sound like thunder cracking—only it wasn't coming from the clouds. It was coming from the street! The ground shook and split open before my eyes.

And I had stopped recording!

"What the heck was that?" I wondered out loud.

The random old lady was right there with the answer: "A crack . . . in the street!"

I went for a closer look as the ground started spraying water. Two rats floated up on a geyser and made me jump.

"Oh, sweetie, you've never seen a rat before?" the random old lady asked me.

One of my best friends is a giant rat, I wanted to say, but didn't. Not when even more rats washed up all around me. There were dozens, maybe hundreds of them.

The old lady ran away, screaming, "AAAHHHH! I've never seen that many rats!"

Me either! They were coming out from everywhere—

potholes, storm drains, and even *the sewers*.

"The sewers must be flooding," I realized. "Oh no! The Turtles! Splinter!"

SPLINTER

I felt like I was being watched.

Which was strange because I was the only one home.

It was rare that I had the sewers to myself. There were always others passing through, making a racket, or ...

... standing right behind me!

I spun around, ready to face an intruder.

Thankfully, it was only a couple of sewer rats, stopping in for a surprise visit. I knew them both. Nice guys, actually.

Where was I? Oh, right ...

The sound of a phone suddenly startled me. It was coming from the boys' room, in Donatello's bunk.

It was his computer ringing. I didn't know much about technology, but I managed to make April's face magically appear on the screen. She looked like she was talking to me from the scene of a monsoon. Her face faded in and out.

"April? I made Donatello's computer work!" I bragged.

"Can you hear me?" she said, breaking up. "The signal is terrible. Are you okay down there? Where are the Turtles?"

"I sent the boys out with their cousins!"

She seemed surprised by this. "Wait—you sent them out . . . into the storm?!"

"It's good for them," I said, expecting her to laugh. But she wasn't in a joking mood. I hadn't seen April this serious in a long time.

"The sewers are flooding," she warned. "I don't think it's safe."

"The sewers are my home. I would never leave them," I said.

And I meant it.

Her image stuttered again. It sounded like she was in the middle of saying "I'm coming to get you," but the computer froze up before she could finish.

"Do not worry about me. I am fine!" I assured her. "Go home, stay dry!"

I never thought I would live to see the day when a

human was worried about *me*. Ha! I was at home, in my slippers, making my special stew.

Besides a few leaks, what was there to worry about?

SPLASH!

That was what I kept hearing on my way back to the kitchen. The sound of running water during a storm wasn't unusual. After all, the lair was getting a bit flooded, and I was making plenty of splashes of my own just walking around.

But the leaks made one specific type of noise, like water pouring out of a pitcher into a glass. Smooth.

These other water sounds I was hearing around the lair were quick . . .

Spli-i-i-ish!

Like water dancing on top of water . . .

Splaaaash!

. . . or someone gliding along it.

Ray, I thought. He's the only mutant I know who can move like that in water.

"Ray Fillet? Is that you?" I foolishly asked out loud.

Of course there was no answer. I shouldn't have expected one. I had sent him out with Raphael and my sweetie, Scumbug.

SPLASH! SPLASH! I heard the sound again.

This was *not* Ray.

My curiosity got the better of me, and I did my best to track the source of the strange sound. I went from room to room, searching. I found nothing out of the ordinary.

"An old man and his imagination," I laughed to myself, heading back to the kitchen.

Then the sound returned . . . this time, with a real *punch.*

SPLISH! SPLASH! WHAM!

Something hit me hard, making the room spin. My vision went fuzzy for a moment, but I swore I was looking at a tiny yellow blur zipping around in front of me.

Then he came into focus. There on the table, in front of me, was a small creature wearing a yellow raincoat and a hat.

A little mutant goldfish.

"I ain't your imagination, old man," he sneered.

For a little fish, this tiny mutant had a lot of power.

The goldfish ran along the top of the floodwater, bouncing off the walls and hitting me with a flurry of punches every time he flew past my nose. I had no choice but to defend myself.

"Mutant, enough!" I said, doing my best to block his speedy strikes.

I tuned out the pain and tried to sense the perfect moment to catch my attacker off guard. My arm snapped out, and I caught him in midair, pinning him against the wall. He was only a little bigger than my paw.

"Stop that!" I said, trying to get him to quit squirming. "Who are you?"

The little troublemaker cut my questions short—with a *slice*! Dozens of mini blades suddenly stuck me at once. I had to drop him.

Before the goldfish vanished back into the water, I saw he had no weapons. Those were his *fins* I'd felt. They must have been as sharp as knives.

I had underestimated this invader. I would not make the same mistake again. I steeled myself and went looking for him.

"Fish?" I called out. "Angry goldfish?"

There were faint sloshing noises from the other room. Almost like footsteps in water!

I ran toward the sound, hoping to surprise him. Only there was no sign of him. Just dripping sounds from the leaks, like a stream. It was still. Calming.

Then, suddenly, a voice startled the shadows. "Splinter!"

"AHHH!" I screamed, turning to attack . . .

. . . when I saw April standing there.

"You scared me half to death!" I gasped. "What are you doing down here?"

"I came to get you out," April said.

"You don't understand—there is a goldfish in here!"

I waited for the realization to dawn on her. Any moment, I knew she'd grasp the seriousness of the danger she was now in.

"Oh, I get it!" April said, totally not getting it. "You know, I had a guinea pig once. You can bring him with us, but we gotta go. Do you need to, like, pack a bag or something? Grab a toothbrush?"

"The goldfish is real! It could still be in the lair!" I warned.

"I'm not going without you!"

"I am not leaving my home!"

I didn't like to put my foot down, but it was important to me that April understand something: *I was staying here. And that was final.*

"Everything good that has ever happened to me has happened here in the sewers," I explained. "I cannot leave."

April looked at me kindly. "Is this about your goldfish?"

Just then, the tiny yellow blur flew out of the water, grabbing my face! "AHHHH!" I screamed.

As I struggled to pry the powerful little mutant off me, I could hear April panicking in the background. Now she got it.

"What the heck?!" I heard her say.

I pulled the fish away and threw him back into the water. No sooner did he splash down than he rocketed straight back up. This time, aiming for April—and barely missing her when she hopped up onto the couch.

"Stay out of the water!" I told her.

The next time the goldfish pounced, I was ready. With ninja focus, I telegraphed his next move, sensing the exact moment he'd leap out of the water.

As he soared through the air, he was met with my kick.

WHAP!

He quickly flew back into the wall, stunned. But before he could slide into the water to regroup, April trapped him . . .

. . . with one of our leaky buckets.

We had caught ourselves a fish.

APRIL

Well, this was news to me: another mutant!

Splinter suggested we move the talking goldfish into an aquarium . . . with a cinder block on top to keep him trapped inside. Probably a good idea. This little guy had a serious temper.

Maybe he'd warm up to some of my questions.

"Excuse me, hey, talking goldfish. . . . What is your deal?" I asked. "Where did you come from? Are you one of Superfly's mutants?"

"The name is Goldfin," he said, unamused. "Not *talking goldfish*."

"Tell us who you are! Why did you attack us? What do you want?"

"You want me to talk? I'll talk. I got all the time in the world."

GOLDFIN

I came from a magical world. One that I'd heard humans call "the East River." It was filled with all sorts of stuff from the surface. Round stuff. Tin stuff. Slimy stuff ungrateful humans threw away.

But it was also filled with families of seahorses, eels, sea anemones, and, yes, goldfish.

We were all different, but we had one thing uniting us as a family: the Jersey Bight Pearl. It was the center of our universe. A shelter from danger. A happy home for our young.

It was everything to us.

Let me guess, you think that sounds like something out of an undersea movie. Like we were all swimming around, singing and dancing with mermaids.

Well, we weren't.

We were just happy to have a place to call our own.

Until one day, the sky fell.

Right on top of me.

It was like a cage of steel. But it was alive, too. Glowing with light and power. I know now it's called a "machine." This machine was sinking fast, and it had me trapped inside. And no matter how hard my friends tried to get me out, I was stuck.

We were doomed.

Just when things were getting dark, I saw a bright light.

The machine was changing—doing something strange to us.

The light mixed with the river and changed everything it touched.

I eventually escaped the machine, but the damage was done. I was different. And so were my friends, who only came to try to save me.

In a blink, we each transformed and took different shapes. We kept our fins and tails, but we also grew arms and legs. We swam, but now we could move like the people on the surface could. We could think. Speak.

And hurt.

We were no longer creatures under the sea.

We became the East River Three.

APRIL

I was mesmerized by Goldfin's tragic backstory.

But tragically: *I wasn't recording! UGH.*

"Could you say that all again?" I asked, reaching for my phone. "So the machine that turned Superfly into Superduperfly transformed you into mutants?"

"You are like our second cousins!" Splinter said cheerily. "We are family!"

Goldfin didn't seem to care. He just stared at the aquarium glass, drawing little circles on it with his fin. "I've come to deliver a warning. We've already dealt with one of your *hero* Turtles. If you don't stay out of our way, we'll take out the rest of them."

His words spooked me. *What did he mean by that? Were the Turtles okay?!*

Splinter gasped. "What have you done?"

Goldfin didn't answer. Instead, he stopped to listen to

a strange drilling sound that was building in the distance somewhere. I heard it, too. It sounded like something was burrowing up from the center of the earth. It shook the sewers like an earthquake.

Like when I saw the pavement crack before.

"What was that?" I asked Splinter, chasing after him to inspect the noise. I followed him to the entrance of the lair as the sound got louder.

"I've heard this before," Splinter said, trying to stay zen. "The last time these tunnels flooded. It's WATER!"

SPLOOOOSH! A wall of water suddenly broke through, rushing straight at us. It all happened so fast, I couldn't react. The walls burst open with water, and I got knocked backward.

The rush washed over me . . .

. . . and took Splinter away in a tidal wave!

"Splinter!" I yelled, coughing up water. But it was too late; he was long gone.

In his place, something bizarre sprouted up. A fleshy vine of some kind . . . Wait—no, not a vine.

A *tentacle*!

Then another. And another. And probably, like, ten more!

A swarm of monstrous things were in the water with me and inching their way closer.

I couldn't believe my eyes—I was face to face with what I can only describe as pink aliens from the deep. They spoke in weird TV quotes—which made the whole situation even creepier.

"Act now! Deals won't last long!"

"Do you or a loved one have irritable bowel syndrome?"

"What are you talking about?" I asked, stunned beyond belief.

"If I had to guess . . . ," I heard a familiar voice say behind me. I turned to see . . .

Goldfin.

He was standing *outside* the fish tank. He'd escaped by cutting a little circle through the glass. "They're saying you're in deep doo-doo."

Goldfin and his gang of mutant weirdoes had me tied up . . . with their tentacles.

It was really gross.

"Look, just let me go, okay?" I pleaded. "I'm no threat to you."

Goldfin wasn't so sure. "If I let you go, you tell everyone about us," he said, beginning to reveal his master plans. "You tell 'em about flooding the city—"

"No, no, no! No need to tell me—"

"About the Natural History Museum—"

"For real. Shut it—"

"You'd tell 'em about our meeting with Bad Bernie at Pier 21."

"I just said I don't need to hear that!" I interrupted for the third time. "I'm not telling anybody anything, okay? You don't have to worry about me or Splinter."

Goldfin glared at me. "I'm not worried about the rat. He'll be sleepin' with the fishes by now."

I knew what he meant by that, but I didn't believe him.

He didn't know Splinter like I did—the rat who didn't like being away from home. Ever.

He'd find his way back. He knew these sewers better than anyone.

SPLINTER

Where was I?

While I was no longer underwater, my head was still swimming . . . with questions.

What part of the sewer was this? And why was I wearing a helmet on my head? I took it off and soon discovered it was no helmet.

It was a crown made of garbage.

Ohhhh no, I realized. *They've gone too far this time!*

My sewer rat friends popped out of the shadows to squeak their greetings and bow. For months they'd been sneaking into the lair to meet with me. They thought I was their king!

It was nice, but also . . . a little bit embarrassing. Believe me, I have tried to tell them many times that I am just a humble ninja master and father of four. But they won't accept this truth. They believe I am their chosen one.

I didn't want the boys, or Scumbug, or April to find out about this. I'd never hear the end of it.

As they showered me with gifts and offerings, I explained to them again: "I am a rat, same as you . . .

except I can talk. And use utensils. You don't need to worship me. Look, my friend April is in trouble—"

They recognized her name. They started anxiously squeaking to each other like they knew something I didn't.

First, they asked if she'd been taken by the crocodile.

"What crocodile?!" I replied.

They changed the subject to inform me they'd heard she was being held prisoner by some pink blobs.

My whiskers lowered in fear. April was in danger, and there wasn't enough time to find the Turtles to help her escape. I needed reinforcements right now.

So I swallowed my pride and addressed my royal subjects: "Your king needs your help."

APRIL

I could tell Goldfin was getting impatient. I needed to stall him while I figured out a way to escape.

"I'm here to tell you . . . no one's coming to save you," Goldfin said, sharpening his fins a little too close to my face.

I looked around the room, scanning for anything I could use as a distraction. That was when I saw something moving in the corner of the lair.

One of the blobby tentacle dudes noticed it, too. "Troubled by pests?" it said, quoting an exterminator commercial.

"What?" Goldfin asked, turning his attention to the walls.

The walls that were now crawling with *rats*! It was an infestation!

And I, for one, loved to see it.

Sewer rats of all shapes and sizes were bursting out of every corner of the room. Some swimming up in the flood, others crawling out of the pipes and vents. They swarmed the tentacle mutants, climbing on top of them!

The mutant weirdoes had no choice but to loosen their grip on me! They needed their tentacles to try to bat the rats away.

I was free! I got away from Goldfin just as a rat dropped from the ceiling onto his fishy face. He screamed, pulling it away . . .

Only to see another set of rat eyes in the darkness behind me.

Higher up than the others, and fiercer—filled with the spirit of a true fighter.

I'd know those eyes anywhere. Splinter had returned!

Goldfin was furious. "You're in my territory now, rat!"

"What you've failed to realize," Splinter said, appearing out of the shadows in a ninja pose, "is that this rat . . . is the deadliest rat there's ever been."

SPLINTER

The pink blobs retreated into the water. My loyal rat subjects had done their duty. Now it was time for me to face the true enemy head-on and defend my home.

I snapped up a discarded umbrella and prepared to strike. While I fended off Goldfin's quick attacks, I remembered training the Turtles when they were only tots. They learned how to use their weapons early—just as effectively as I was using mine now.

The boys would laugh, trying to dodge my practice swings. I could almost hear their little voices, giggling. And see myself marking their heights on the wall.

This is what I was fighting for. This is why I could never leave this place.

Goldfin said he wanted a home, but I wasn't sure he knew what *home* truly means. A home is more than a place. A home is made of memories you create and share with those who matter to you.

I wasn't going to let Goldfin take that from me.

I surprised Goldfin with a swift kick that sent him flying back. I could see his frustration building. He knew he was losing this battle—so he tried one last desperate act to win. He went after someone else.

He lunged at April, pulling her down into the water with him! I couldn't let him get away.

The fish spun his fin-blades like a fan, creating a vortex of swirling water he could use to vanish them both down into the depths. He was moving quickly—I couldn't hesitate.

I dove in.

Ninja Tip: Go with the flow. Especially when you're in water.

Goldfin's spin was sucking in everything around him, like a whirlpool. So, using all my focus and concentration, I simply went with the flow, letting the spinning force pull me straight to its center!

Directly to Goldfin's face!

With my fist!

KA-POWWW! I hit him so hard, he set sail ... out of the water and across my living room. He hit the wall in a daze.

As for April? I rescued her just in time. She coughed up water and caught her breath. "I would do anything for my family," I told her, "including you."

When I got up to find another bucket to trap our fishy friend, I discovered he was gone! Judging by the stillness of the water, I knew he was no longer in the lair with us.

He was out there, somewhere. Ready to cause more trouble, no doubt.

"We have to find him," I told April. "My boys are still in danger."

"Well, we know where he's going to be," she said.

"We do?"

"Yeah, he wouldn't shut up about it ... the Natural History Museum and the pier."

I looked ahead, determined to go. I wasn't abandoning this place but merely stepping out for a little while.

I was going to find my boys and bring them home.

CHAPTER 4
GOLDFIN

That wasn't the first time I'd been kicked out of someone's home. A few weeks ago, I'd been thrown out of another home—*mine*.

I remember it like it was yesterday.

Me and the rest of the East River Three—the seahorse, Mustang Sally; Lee the Eel; and some sea anemones—were pushed out of the water . . .

. . . by our own families!

They didn't recognize us. Not after the *change*. Our fellow fish couldn't see past our newly grown arms and legs. All they saw were freaks of nature.

Monsters that weren't welcome at the Pearl anymore.

Heartbroken, we crawled up on the shore and found a place underneath the pier. It wasn't cozy, but it was something. We had shelter from the elements, a TV to help us pass the time, and, of course, a view of the river.

I'd look out at the water and think, *At least our families will be okay. They may not have us anymore, but they still have a home. And as a parent, that's all that really matters.*

Then the machines came. Not like the one that transformed us. These machines were bigger. They had scoopers on the end of them, and they were able to stay on dry land but somehow dig into the ocean with the push of a button.

Men in yellow hard hats controlled them. They didn't seem friendly to outsiders, but they were very happy in their machines.

Especially on the day they scooped a massive rock from the river—the biggest one they'd ever seen.

My heart broke again.

It was the Pearl.

DONATELLO

Whenever the weather got bad and our internet went out, it meant I was going out, too. Out of my bunk, out of the lair, and out to fix the signal so Dad could stream his shows without interruption.

I usually made these Turtle tech support runs on my own, but since the Mutanimals were bunking with us, I had a buddy. A very anxious buddy.

Wingnut.

The deeper we went into the sewer tunnels, the more her bat wings scraped against the ceiling. I guess it made her feel like the walls were closing in on us.

I tried to take her mind off things with some tech talk, but it was no use. She was too busy looking over her shoulder at *every . . . little . . . noise.*

"Do you ever feel like you're being followed?" she asked.

"Probably just the construction Raph was talking about," I said, hoping that would calm her down.

It didn't. It was time for plan B.

B for *bananas.*

I brought them to share with the rats down here, but

I didn't think they would mind if I gave my friend one.

"Want a banana?" I asked.

"I can't. They trigger my gag reflex," she revealed. "It started after my transformation. I used to love bananas."

"That's fascinating, and sad, I guess? Maybe mash them up?"

"YOU THINK I HAVEN'T TRIED THAT?!" Wingnut suddenly snapped.

No, she wasn't going bananas. Her anxiety was clearly getting the best of her. And to be honest, it was kinda starting to rub off on me. I felt like I was breathing a little heavier than usual, and I wasn't even claustrophobic. I was just panicking because she was panicking.

She quickly apologized. "Sorry, it's just—it's like I can't breathe. And it's dark. Why is it so dark?"

"You're in a sewer," I said. "Historically, they're dark. There's nothing to be afraid of."

GOLDFIN

"The Jersey Bight is thought to be one of the biggest pearls in the world...."

That was how the humans on TV talked about the Pearl.

They showed pictures of it—and we couldn't believe it. It had gone through a transformation, just like us.

But the Pearl changed in a different way. It was now clean and smooth. All the layers of life that had built up on it over generations had been washed away, revealing a bright white ball underneath.

The humans put the Pearl in a giant glass box, in a place called "the Natural History Museum."

History! I had to laugh. *That's exactly what the humans took from us!*

And now our families were out there in the river, without protection, lost at sea.

I couldn't bear the thought of it.

On that day, I made a vow to steal it back.

I tried convincing Mustang Sally and Lee the Eel to join me. "Think about it: we return home with the Pearl, and we'll be welcomed back as heroes."

Back then, they didn't want to listen.

But like the Pearl in the glass box, they'd soon see the light.

DONATELLO

Aaaah! We finally breathed a little easier. We'd squeezed out of the tight access tunnels and waded into the more open spaces of the electrical junction. This was the nerve center for power and internet for the lair.

It was like *the great outdoors,* but you know . . . underground. And for nerds.

But still great!

All I had to do was recalibrate this bad boy, and we'd be good to go. "We'll be finished in no time," I told Wingnut. "Then we can go outside and maybe play bocce with Leatherhead."

"Have you noticed anything different about Leatherhead lately?" Wingnut asked, sounding a little concerned about our mutual mutant friend. "She's not fitting in."

"Hey, I get it. She's an Australian in New York. Not to mention the whole mutant crocodile thing."

Wingnut proceeded to tell me why she was worried about Leatherhead. That she'd snooped on her search history—which kinda shocked me. She told me that she discovered Leatherhead had been searching for articles on de-mutation.

This really shocked me.

"Is that even possible?" Wingnut asked me.

If it were, it'd be a bombshell, I thought.

At that moment, something big exploded past us like a freight train. Some kind of mystery object barreled down the tunnels, kicking up floodwater.

"What was that?!" I said, shaking it off.

Wingnut looked like she had seen a ghost.

Or something worse.

"It was a . . . giant MONSTER!" she screamed.

It couldn't be. Monsters that big were usually only in kaiju movies. She was seeing things.

I felt the floor tremble beneath our feet, like an aftershock. I could hear what sounded like a jackhammer in the distance. I tried to steady myself . . .

. . . when everything crumbled.

In an instant, the ground collapsed underfoot, taking me and Wingnut down in one swift fall. We screamed all the way down, the walls closing in on us until we finally hit rubble.

Debris rained down on top of us.

We had fallen into an ancient tunnel system deep underground, with no visible way out.

Wingnut wasn't going to want to hear this, but . . . the walls had closed in on us again.

WINGNUT

FREAKING OUT!

I tried stretching my wings, but there was nowhere for them to move. I tried getting some personal space, but the walls had squeezed us together like sardines.

"I—I—I have to get out of here," I said through chattering teeth.

"Wingnut, you have to chill!" I could hear Donnie say. "You're making things worse!"

HOW COULD THIS GET ANY WORSE?!

"There is a giant monster down here with us," I reminded him. My heart was pounding, and my wings were trembling.

"Whatever that thing was, it's gone," Donnie assured me. "We're going to find a way out of here."

I didn't believe him. Not when the water was leaking through the ceiling and the walls were rising up all around us. Fast.

If the water didn't get us, then the monster would.

Even in the dark, I could see its shadow circling us. This was not a hallucination. The monster was real, and it was way too close for comfort.

I spotted its two eyes watching us.

Then I saw its teeth. Lots and lots of teeth.

FREAKING OUT, FREAKING OUT, FREAKING OUT . . .

DONATELLO

I squinted. The thing in the water with us was big, no doubt. But it was not the freight train-sized monster-thing I'd seen back in the tunnels. This was something else.

I looked closer. I'd know that scaly face anywhere.

"That's not a monster," I observed. "It's a crocodile."

Wingnut took another look. "Oh no! Leatherhead!" She gasped. "She de-mutated! But how?"

I racked my brain. If this indeed was her, there was only one possible scientific explanation. "The T.C.R.I. tranquilizers!" I deduced, remembering the same serum-blasting weapons we'd used to shrink Superduperfly down to size. "But how could she have gotten one?"

"Maybe she broke into their lab?" Wingnut guessed.

"Yeah, and she was all . . . *Oi, mate, give me one of those mutatizing blasters*," I said, doing my best-worst Australian accent. *"Or I'mma eat ya like a dingo!"*

"That's a terrible impression!" Wingnut scoffed, about to do her own silly imitation of Leatherhead's voice.

But the croc snapped at us, startling us into silence!

We managed to crawl up the pile of debris behind us, using it almost like a rock wall. We were out of the water but not out of harm's way. The croc reared up, trying to turn us into a snack.

We used what we could. While I whopped its jaw with my bo staff, Wingnut stole my bananas and threw them at the beast.

Believe it or not, her plan actually worked for a sec! The croc started choking. "Bananas triggered her gag reflex," Wingnut said, humblebragging.

You learn something new every day.

"The only chance we have of getting out is to reason with her," Wingnut added, getting serious now. "Our friend is in there somewhere."

SNAP! The croc chomped again. Not friendly. Not at all.

"You're not thinking logically," I said. "Eventually, my

brothers will realize we're missing, and they'll come. We just have to hold tight. We've got the high ground."

As if on cue, Wingnut got her wing stuck in one of the pipes and resumed freaking out all over again. We managed to pry it loose, but the damage was done: her wing had somehow punctured the pipes above, and the water shot out faster now, filling up the chamber.

Lifting the croc even closer to us.

CHOMP! We dodged the croc again—barely.

"Maybe Leatherhead was right," Wingnut said, suddenly overcome with sadness. "I just want to be a tiny bat again and fly away."

That hit me hard. I didn't want to lose *another* mutant cousin. "I'm sorry, I'm not good at this whole *feelings* thing."

Wingnut clearly needed to talk through her emotions, but my brain just wasn't wired like that. I needed to find a way to communicate with her in a way we both understood.

Nerd stuff.

I brought up some of our favorite anime and sci-fi movies. Specifically the ones where characters get trapped—just like we were.

Wingnut got all my movie references right away, snapping out of her panic to quote her favorite lines back at me.

My plan was working.

Her attitude completely changed. She even offered up a geeky example of her own. "What about when Superfly had you and your brothers and was squeezing you so hard your shells cracked?"

"Good one." I laughed. "Wanna know what those all had in common?"

"They were terrifying?" Wingnut guessed.

"Everyone got out alive," I told her. "And we will, too."

Wingnut gently smiled. "Thanks, Donnie. Wow, I feel better!"

WHOOOSH!

The croc suddenly struck, surprising us both. It clamped down hard on Wingnut's metal arm, dragging her back into the water with it. Ugh, just when she was finally calming down!

"Oh, come on!" I shouted.

The time for talking was over. Now was the moment to take action.

I needed to wrestle a crocodile.

"Donnie!" Wingnut yelled.

I needed to act fast. Wingnut's metal arm was strong enough to protect against the croc's bite, but for how long?

Maybe I needed something metal, too. *Think, Donnie, think.*

Logic.

Some rebar rods were poking out from the rocks—those would definitely be stronger than my wooden bo staff. Using all my strength, I yanked a rod free and dove in after Wingnut.

"Donnie!" I heard her yell again. The beast was moving fast, sinking deeper into the dark. I had to make my move now or risk losing Wingnut forever.

Kicking my feet, I lunged forward like a Turtle torpedo. I soon closed the gap—rebar sticking out ahead like a sword—and jabbed the croc right in its side!

Direct hit!

The crocodile released its grip, and I snatched

Wingnut away, carrying her back toward our rocks at the head of the chamber.

As I pulled us back up onto dry land, we both breathed a sigh of relief.

"We need to move," I said. "We can't stay here any longer."

I looked at the rebar in my hand. There was a ton of this stuff poking out of the walls. If the rods were strong enough to hold off the croc, maybe they'd be strong enough to hold us up, too.

We were able to use the rebar like a ladder to climb up into a larger chamber, where we could finally stretch our legs. No more walls, just the wide-open spaces of the sewers I knew.

The best part: Wingnut could stretch her wings without having to worry about bringing down the ceiling!

"Donnie, I don't know what I would have done without you down here," she said, gratefully.

I'd guess we got about . . . oh, *thirty seconds of*

calm . . . before the waters near us started stirring.

"She's following us! How is that even possible?!" Wingnut squeaked. "Logically doesn't make any sense."

Wingnut shot me a look that said *what now?*

I was all out of ideas. Logic and rebar had gotten us this far, but it clearly wasn't enough. The croc would soon be within snacking distance again. I needed to try a different approach.

"This whole time I've been trying to use logic to get us out," I said, realizing what had to be done. "Logic ain't getting us out of this corner. I need to do this on a reptilian level. On instinct. Right brain style."

I waded back into the water. I could see the croc swimming toward me in the dark.

"If Leatherhead's in there, I can connect with her," I said. "We're friends."

I waded in farther, ignoring everything in my left brain telling me to *RUN. GET OUT OF THERE. LOOK AT THE SIZE OF THIS THING!*

"Leatherhead, it's me Donnie. Are you in there?" I said, trying my best to remain calm.

I saw the croc's head pop up. *Like it was listening.*

All I had to do was speak to her. Like I knew her. Just like I had done with Wingnut before.

Nerd stuff.

"Remember all those hours we spent ranking fictitious reptiles?" I asked, trying to jog her memory. "You said the Loch Ness Monster was underrated, remember?"

I remembered. I had our whole list memorized.

I started to run though our complete list of favorite monsters, puppets, and cryptids.

"It's working!" Wingnut said, noticing the croc begin to relax.

The vibe was definitely calmer in the chamber now. We were connecting.

And then, something incredible happened.

The croc spoke to me.

I heard her say, "Donatello . . . ?"

But it sounded like she was talking from far away, in the shadows, even though she was right here. *Huh?*

"Wait," I said, suddenly clocking *two* different shadows.

Stupefied, I looked across the water as a familiar face emerged from the side of the chamber. My eyes widened.

I was finally looking at the *real* Leatherhead.

Across the room.

"But if you're over there, then—"

I looked back to the creature approaching me. It wasn't a crocodile, it was an alligator. And the gator *wasn't* my friend. The gator didn't care about nerdy lists.

It only cared about turning me into a meal.

I screamed!

The only thing tougher than rebar? My shell!

The gator clamped down on it, and I didn't feel a thing. I mean, except fear. I definitely felt *a lot* of fear.

The beast pulled me into the water, but I was able to wiggle myself out of its jaws and run back to the shore.

"That was terrifying," I said, trying to catch my breath. "We need a plan. I tried connecting with it, and that was a terrible idea."

"What did I miss?" Leatherhead asked.

"We thought you were de-mutated," Wingnut told her.

"I was on a walkabout when I ran into my own kind

down here," Leatherhead explained. "I thought it was maybe a sign that I shouldn't be a mutant anymore."

"What happened?" I asked her.

She stepped into the light, revealing she was injured. "Stupid alligator bit me, didn't it? The whole group of them were quite unpleasant. I think I'm ready to accept being a mutant."

Finally, some good news. Leatherhead was here to stay.

Since we were talking about acceptance . . .

"I need to accept I'm not like my brothers," I added. "I'm me. I'm left-brained, and I need to have faith in that."

"You got any ideas, then?" Leatherhead asked, pointing at the shadow gliding through the water. "'Cause that thing is circling us again."

Before I could say anything, Wingnut came forward with an announcement of her own. "I've got an idea."

Leatherhead and I looked at her, impressed. The anxious bat girl we knew didn't seem freaked out in this moment. She seemed determined. And tired of running.

"Lend me your wrench," Wingnut said.

I knew what she was thinking.

Tools. Logic. We were about to drop some science.

With a little recalibration here and some basic robotics there, we worked together to turn Wingnut's metal arm into a serious sci-fi contraption that belonged in an anime . . .

. . . or the inside of a gator's mouth.

"What are you gonna do with that?" Leatherhead asked, trying to figure out what our invention was.

"We're gonna shut this gator's trap once and for all," I answered. "By keeping it open!"

Wingnut and I proudly presented the Metal Muzzle . . . aka the Gator Gag.

Time for the field test. I swallowed my fear and dove back into the water.

The gator was on me right away, charging—opening its jaws nice and wide.

I released the muzzle and pushed it into the gator's mouth. The trap was set. All I needed now was to let the gator do what came naturally. . . .

Bite.

The second the beast clamped down, the Metal Muzzle clicked right into place. The gator's eyes widened, sensing something was very wrong. It bucked back and forth in a rage, trying to spit the contraption out.

But it couldn't.

The gator couldn't shut its jaws, which meant we had shut the beast down!

Leatherhead and Wingnut cheered. I followed the beast as it crawled out of the water and up onto dry land, seeming to give up in defeat. It even let out this totally sad groan, which was hilarious.

Yeah, it was all fun and games . . .

. . . until another huge shadow suddenly lunged out of the water, nearly biting us in half.

Another gator!

It was Leatherhead who leapt into action this time. Even though she was hurting, she made it look easy. With one throw, she grabbed this new gator by its snout, flipping it onto its back.

I raced toward them, expecting to have to make another DIY muzzle on the fly, but there was no need. The gator was fast asleep. It looked like Raph after eating a whole pizza—just this green lump passed out on the ground.

It didn't make sense. "What in the world?" I wondered aloud.

"Ya just flip her over, mate," Leatherhead explained, like it was no big deal. "Cuts off the blood supply to the noggin. She'll have a nice li'l kip."

Crocodile logic.

I sighed. "We really could have used that information earlier!"

We headed back through the tunnels the way we had come, catching up and hearing all about Leatherhead's travels. Then she got serious for a moment. "You know there's another mutant out there, right? Some kind of snake or eel creature."

"That's what trapped us down here!" I said.

"And I assume it did *that*," Wingnut added, pointing ahead at a wall of rubble now blocking off the tunnel. I could hear strange sounds coming from the other side.

"You hear that?" I asked.

"What if it's the eel?" Wingnut said with worry. "What do we do?"

"Hide!"

We all stepped back, clinging to the shadows as the rubble began to fall away. Something was coming through.

We each picked up a rock, just in case we needed something heavy to throw at whatever we were about to meet.

Lucky for us, they were our kind of creatures.

"Raph?!" I exclaimed.

Not just Raph—but Ray Fillet and Scumbug, too! The three of them climbed through the rubble. But they didn't look overjoyed to see us. In fact, they looked more panicked than we did.

Raph came running up to me. "Donnie! We're in trouble, man."

Funny. I was about to say the same exact thing to him.

CHAPTER 5
LEONARDO

When you're the leader of the Ninja Turtles, there's no job too big or too small. Like right now . . . it may appear that I was merely taking a giant pigeon out for a walk, but there was a lot more to it than that.

Pigeons need guidance. Especially mutant ones like Pigeon Pete. Even though he was Michelangelo's creation, this six-foot-tall pigeon had become my problem.

I mean, my *student.* Pete had become my student.

You see, Dad charged me with looking out for him. Why? Well, because Pete was basically a giant baby. But also because I am the responsible one! Because I'm a natural born leader. It's like I always say . . .

"You are a natural born leader, with a bold, commanding presence that people can't help but follow. They respect you, and *maybe* fear you a little, too. But most importantly, they listen to you."

I said all that out loud, and Pete wasn't even listening! He was just digging his beak into his feathers again.

"PETE? Will you just listen to me?" I said, trying to get his attention. "We're supposed to go get some air."

I was high up on the ladder that would lead us topside, to the surface. But we weren't close to leaving. Pete hadn't even stepped onto the bottom rung yet.

"C'mon, we have to go up!" I pleaded, watching Pete peck around. "PETER! No, don't eat that—"

I wanted to shake some sense into Pete, but something else did it for me!

The sewers suddenly rumbled around us. Was it an earthquake? It shook me so hard, I lost my grip and slid down.

"SQUAWK!" Pete sounded like an alarm. He flapped his wings frantically, pointing at the wall—almost like he saw something that spooked him.

Spooked him enough to finally get his bird butt up the ladder.

He was pushing me up toward the surface now, as if he was trying to get ahead of me. "Pete, wait!" I said. But there was no talking him down.

He pushed harder, and my head wound up lifting the manhole cover. Water instantly flooded in, splashing me right in the face.

"For real, this is a terrible idea," I said, popping my head out to look around the rainy streets. Pete followed my lead and popped his head out, too.

We were jammed up, squeezed side by side, like a two-headed monster barely able to fit through the manhole. Pete's wings flapped on my head. "Will you stop that?"

"SQUAWK!" Pete squawked.

"Why do I always get saddled with you?"

Pete kept pushing, and flapping, and trying to get free.

I held my position. I was trying to make sure it was safe for us to leave, but if he wanted out so bad, fine. I couldn't take it anymore. "You know what? Go get some air. I don't care!"

I made room for Pete to go topside, and the moment he flew past me, he caught some air, all right.

The winds had totally swept him away!

I popped my head back out of the manhole and saw Pigeon Pete tumbling through the air like some kind of bird balloon. His squawk echoed off the buildings. *"SQUAAAWWWWK!"*

"Whoops," I said, realizing I'd just made a huge mistake.

Maybe now was the time not to lead but to follow.

Follow that pigeon!

Ever chased a runaway kite? Or a balloon that got loose?

Yeah, this was about a million times worse.

Pigeon Pete was big and dense, so every time he collided with something, he made a pretty big dent. He'd fly into a window and smash it. The wind would throw him through some treetops, and he'd make it rain broken branches. He bounced off car hoods and street umbrellas and was somehow causing more damage than the actual storm.

All I could do was try to keep up with him from the street and not get flattened by flying objects.

"Peter, stop!" I shouted in my best dad voice. "You get down from there right now, young man!"

He flapped, but no luck. The wind pushed him higher and farther.

I leapt over a downed trash can, trying to keep pace, but a falling branch knocked me down into a puddle, face-first.

I looked at my reflection in the water. I didn't look good at all. "Some leader you are, man. People are supposed to listen to you."

To my shock, my reflection suddenly melted away.

The puddle was draining . . . into a crack in the pavement. A long, huge crack that kept growing and branching out. This was *definitely not* normal.

I stood up, startled—just as the rumbling returned.

The ground shook violently and made the crack even wider. I watched it tear through the concrete, up onto the sidewalk. *FLOOOM!* It made a fire hydrant explode into a geyser of water!

Some invisible disaster was happening under the city. I had never seen anything like it. "Okay, this is not good. I gotta get back to the lair. I gotta tell my brothers."

ONCE TROUBLEMAKING ENEMIES, the Mutanimals are now trusted Turtle allies.

LEATHERHEAD is a giant Australian crocodile. She likes to help the Turtles, but she's not always happy in New York. Sometimes she wants to leave the city life behind and wander off on walkabout.

Low-key and a little sarcastic, GENGHIS FROG seems to attract chaos. But when he's focused on something—especially food—it's almost impossible to stop him.

WINGNUT is a bat who's afraid of the dark, doesn't really love sewers, and gets a little claustrophobic at times.

She's happiest with the Turtles, especially Donatello. A fellow mechanical genius, Wingnut can talk to him nonstop about tech, anime, and comic books.

RAY FILLET is a mutant manta ray who loves to sing. Sometimes he's hard to understand—and a little off pitch—but he's always in tune with his Turtle teammates when it matters most.

SCUMBUG spends most of her time with the Turtles because she *really* likes their father and sensei, Splinter. Even though she means well, the brothers are conflicted. Scumbug's squeaky vermin speech is hard to understand, and she tends to vomit a lot.

Wait, I remembered, stopping myself. I couldn't get into hero mode. Not when Pete was still on the loose.

I looked up through the sheets of rain, but there was no sign of him anywhere. Just black clouds.

"How am I ever gonna find him in this?" I sighed.

That was when I heard someone yell a few streets over. "A giant mutant pigeon!"

"Never mind," I told myself, "I guess it's not that hard."

I found Pete.

All I had to do was go toward the sirens.

He'd managed to come back down to earth . . . right on top of a cop car. He'd crushed it and was flapping his wings in the faces of two very angry police officers.

"SQUAWK!" Pete bellowed.

"It's attacking us!" one cop said. "Take it down!"

"No!" I yelled, pulling Pete off the cops. "He's not attacking; he's not trying to hurt you. He's just . . . I don't know . . . confused, maybe?"

"COOO! COOO!" Pete cooed.

"You're not helping here, Pete."

Pete freaked out again and attempted to fly away. Fortunately, I grabbed him before he could blast off. "Pete, stop!"

But I couldn't hold him down anymore. My feet lifted off the ground.

I was going for a ride.

More cops arrived on the scene. One officer—clearly the guy in charge—saw past the feathers and the goofy beak; he looked like he was seeing a monster in the flesh for the first time ever.

He stared up at us with his mouth open in disgust . . .

. . . just as Pete nervously pooped on him.

It went *everywhere*. The guy's coat. Face. Even inside his mouth.

I heard him scream.

I'd always dreamed of what it would be like to fly over the city like a superhero.

Now I knew . . . it was a nightmare!

We were so high up . . . and everything was coming at us so, so fast.

I held on to Pete's leg for dear life as we nearly crashed through billboards and water towers. If I didn't know any better, I'd have thought he was trying to knock me off!

Maybe Pete wanted an apology. "I'm sorry about what I said," I told him. "Just don't drop me. This isn't cool!"

"COOOO!" Pete cooed at me, as if he was trying to communicate something important. But I didn't understand him.

He flew us back over the streets, like he was tracking something way down in the flood. I thought I saw a shape swimming around down there, but I was probably just imagining it. Everything looked weird from this height.

Especially that crack in the ground.

"Stop messing around, we have to go back!" I pleaded. "Will you listen to me for once?"

I tried "driving" Pete by turning his leg where I

wanted him to go, but that only made him mad. He flapped and fought me, still wanting to follow the flood.

Eventually, he got tired and stopped flapping altogether. Right as the wind and the rain randomly calmed down, too.

It took me a hot sec to realize *we were falling*.

"AHHHHH!" I screamed as we plummeted down toward the ground.

The world was moving up at me like a blur—I had no idea where we were about to crash-land. The flood? The trees? Splat on the ground somewhere?

I braced myself. . . .

And we fell through a roof, into a warehouse filled with fog.

No, not fog. *Steam.*

I got to my feet and saw pipes all around us. We were in an industrial building with valves and gauges as far as the eye could see. I shook off the flight, got my bearings, and clocked a sign through the steam up ahead. . . .

MIDTOWN WATER PUMP STATION

Pete had flown us into the place where all the water in the city flowed. Like there wasn't enough water outside! That silly Pete.

Pete!

Where is he? I wondered. I looked around for him, but once again, he was gone. I was about to panic, when I heard a *"COOO–OOO–OO!"* echo nearby.

Above me.

It was Pete cooing from the rafters. He was perched next to a flock of normal pigeons. *"COOO!"*

"Coo? That's seriously all you have to say for yourself?" I said, relieved to see he was alive. Well, somewhat relieved.

Pete started aggressively flapping his wings again. Like he was trying to warn me about something. *"COOOO!"*

I scanned the place to see what he was freaking out about, but all I saw were hissing pipes. That was no big deal. I was pretty sure that happened all the time in a place filled with nothing but pipes.

"COOOO!" Pete cooed again, flapping his wings out like he was pointing at something behind me.

I followed his gaze, turning around to see a dark shape cloaked within the steam.

Someone else was in here with us!

This mysterious giant came closer, slowly revealing itself to be . . .

A mutant seahorse!

"You made a big mistake coming here," the seahorse said.

I nodded. "Yeah, I was about to say that."

A few of the pipes nearby began rattling, like they were about to bust. I didn't know this mutant, but I thought it was worth bringing up that this place was a ticking time bomb. "Hey, I think there's something wrong here. . . . We have to get out!"

The seahorse disagreed with me. Know how I knew?

He threw a punch at my head. Then another! I was in a fight, and I wasn't ready. Instincts kicked in, and I dodged and moved to higher ground.

My mutant attacker couldn't reach me up this high.

Not without a weapon. *Which he had.*

Through the steam, I could see the seahorse pull out a slingshot. He popped a barnacle shell into the slot and fired. *THUMP!* It nailed me right between my eyes.

Honestly, it was a great shot. Not that I would've told him that. I was too busy falling backward into a water

tank with my eyes rolling around in my skull.

SPLAAASH!

The hot water woke me up, snapping me out of my daze.

So this was how we were gonna do this? Slingshots and shell games? Well, I had something just as powerful and surprising up my sleeve, too.

My katanas.

I popped up from the water and . . . *Slash!* I lunged toward him, going to town with my blades, but the swords weren't doing any damage whatsoever. I swung harder, but that didn't change anything.

I looked at the seahorse in shock—I wasn't even making a scratch! I might as well have been fighting with a plastic fork.

"Hey! Be careful!" the seahorse said, stopping to talk.

I froze. "What?"

"You could sprain a wrist or something. My armor's pretty tough."

To say I was dumbfounded would be an understatement. "Now you suddenly care about me getting hurt? You're attacking me!"

"Yeah, well . . . you came here to stop me."

"Stop you from what?! I don't even know who you are!"

The seahorse posed menacingly, staring me dead in the eyes. "My name is Mustang Sally, and I'm a soon-to-be parent trying to give my babies a better life."

My eyes practically bulged out of my head. "You're having a baby?"

"Babies, *plural*," Mustang Sally clarified. "Like, hundreds of them. That's how seahorses roll."

Man, I really need to visit the aquarium more. Indestructible body armor. Mad parenting skills. Who knew seahorses were this interesting?

I lowered my swords and ignored the rattling pipes for a moment. If there was a time for questions, I was pretty sure it was right now.

"Where did you come from? What do you even want?" I asked.

"We just want to go home, man," Mustang Sally answered. "We came from the river, under the safety of the Jersey Bight Pearl. But Goldfin found a way for us to go home again. . . . The East River Three are going to take back what's ours!"

Not gonna lie, I had no idea what any of that meant.

"Goldfin? Who is—?"

"*COOO!*" Pigeon Pete interrupted me, still cooing from the rafters.

"Pete! Get down from there!" I shouted back. I gestured up at Pete and let Sally know: "I came here to get that guy, then I'm out of your hair. Or fin. Or . . . whatever you've got going on."

"Really? You're not trying to stop me?" Sally asked, confused.

"No! I don't even know what you're doing, honestly," I assured him. "But for real, I think this place is gonna blow up, and we should probably all go."

"*SQUAWWWWK!*" Pete squawked over the hissing sounds coming from the pipes.

"What's his problem?" Mustang Sally asked.

"Yeah, sorry about him. He's only been a mutant for a few weeks," I explained. "I guess he's just having a hard time adjusting."

WOOP! WOOP! Sirens suddenly wailed. Then there were red and blue lights bouncing off the windows. A voice boomed from a bullhorn outside.

"Attention, Demon Pigeon! This is the police! We have

the building surrounded! Come out with your hands or wings or whatever UP!"

Pete squawked again. He sounded more frantic and was clearly pointing at the cops outside.

"Or maybe he was trying to warn us about *that*," Mustang Sally said.

Sally and I peeked out through the window. We were surrounded by every cop in the city—including the one Pete had pooped on. He was the man covered in white goop, on the bullhorn. "You have five minutes to comply!" he announced.

"Five minutes," Mustang Sally said, thinking. "That's plenty of time."

"To get out of here?" I asked, hopeful.

"No, to blow this place up."

I took a big step back, very aware of the pipes hissing and the pressure gauges spiking. "You're the one doing all this? Why?"

"Pump station was my job," Sally said, coming clean about their plan. "Lee's was the tunneling. . . . I gotta mess with this place so it'll flood the museum. And Midtown, too."

"COOO!" I heard Pete sound off from the rafters. It was different from his usual cooing, more like the crazed noises he'd made during the flight over here.

When he was tracking the floods.

That was when it hit me. Pete wasn't being his normal birdbrained self—he had been trying to warn me *this whole time.*

I picked up my katanas. "I can't let you do this."

Sally surprised me again . . . by putting a tender hand on my shoulder. Like a parent would. "If you were my baby, I'd be so proud of you right now!" Then his eyes narrowed. "But you're not."

Mustang Sally suddenly turned on me, lifting me off the ground.

Even with the steam forming around us, I could see he was *fuming.*

Pigeon Pete flew to my rescue.

Well, *flapped* is more like it.

It all happened so quick. There was a burst of feathers, and then I was back on my own two feet. Pete had dropped down and was flapping his wings in Sally's face until he let go—

Then he tackled me.

Just as the cops fired tranquilizer darts through the windows. A hit from one of those would have knocked any of us out cold. We'd have been as good as captured.

Pete had saved me from danger *again*!

Now I was the one who felt like a proud parent. I stared into Pete's beady pigeon eyes. "You actually did that on purpose," I said, grateful. "This whole time, you knew!"

"SQUAWK!" Pete said.

It was a lot sweeter than it sounds.

I could hear the cops barging in through the pump station's doors. Time was ticking. The whole building was shaking. Water was leaking from every crack and crevice.

If I wanted to live long enough to properly potty train Pete, I'd need to track Sally down before he could complete his evil plan.

I headed back into the steam, scanning ... searching ...

Then I saw him shutting the rest of the pumps down. He wasn't kidding—that seriously would flood Midtown! It was already flooding the building. The water was up to my ankles.

Now it was my turn to spring into action. I surprised Sally with a flying kick, knocking him away from the pump controls! *WHAP!*

Sally picked himself up and stared us down. "Not smart, kid. Now you and the bird have to pay."

We both froze, spotting cops coming through the steam.

"You called the cops?" Sally asked.

"Sally, you don't have to do this!" I pleaded. "We can help you!"

"You know what your problem is? You don't listen! I'll do what I have to do for my kids."

Sally dove, vanishing into the water. I went after him, hearing some commotion up ahead.

Through the steam, I could see the shadows of the

cops swarming. One by one, the clueless officers were dropping like flies. *SPLISH! SPLASH!* Something was stealthily attacking them from the shadows, pulling them down into the water. Something tall and fast.

It had to be Sally. He was too speedy for me to make my move without getting ambushed.

I figured my best play would be to try to save the last cop. The one with the bullhorn, who smelled like poop. "Come on, you demon bird!" I heard him say. "Where are you?!"

Right before Sally could pounce, I made my move . . . and tackled the Bird Poop Cop out of the way, just in the nick of time!

He was safe from Sally, but I wasn't.

The mutant seahorse came after me with everything he had. Punches. Kicks. Tail swipes. I blocked and dodged and tried to talk some sense into him. "All the water in the city comes through here. If you don't stop, it's gonna blow!"

"It's the only way!" Mustang Sally said, taking another tail swipe at me.

"Innocent people are going to get hurt!" I said, trying to make him understand.

"COO COOO!" Pete suddenly flew over us toward the rafters.

The Bird Poop Cop didn't notice us in the steam—not yet. He had his sights set on Pete and Pete only. This guy had a one-track mind.

He aimed a mini cannon and fired—*BAM!*—unleashing an electrified net that spun through the air. It knocked Pete down into a water tank, shocking him senseless with powerful volts.

I had a difficult choice to make—stay and capture Sally or try to save Pete.

Pete was my responsibility, so I knew what had to be done.

"PETE!" I yelled. "I'm coming, buddy!"

I ran to my friend, hoping I wasn't too late. I found him unconscious but still buzzing from the electrical shocks. I cut the sparking net off him. "Pete, you gotta wake up, man. You can poop anywhere you want."

There was no answer. Just twitching.

"Please," I begged. "You gotta be okay!"

Finally, Pete cooed. It was like music to my ears.

He started to wake up. He blinked his eyes open and said, "Thank you."

"Yeah, no problem. Maybe we can still stop this," I answered, before realizing *I could suddenly understand Pete!*

"You can talk?!" I gasped.

"Yeah, I suppose," he answered.

"When did that happen?!"

KABLAM! A few pipes burst, and water came rushing out of them.

"Know what? Maybe we put a pin in this for now," I said, remembering we had bigger things to deal with.

Including the Bird Poop Cop, who I could hear radioing for backup. "We need to take him into custody!"

Pete's eyes bulged. We couldn't chase Sally *and* save the city *and* take on the cops all at the same time. We needed to get the police off our trail.

But how?

"Coo cooo cooo . . . ," I heard. Like a sign from above.

I looked up and saw that Pete's pigeon friends were

still up in the rafters, avoiding the chaos below.

I had an idea. "The cops want a pigeon? We'll give them a pigeon."

From the safety of the air, Pete and I quietly watched as the cops made a shocking discovery. . . .

There, floating on the net, on top of the water . . . was the notorious Demon Pigeon they'd been chasing all night. A completely normal-sized New York City pigeon.

I set the bird there myself.

The cops looked at the Bird Poop Cop with disgust.

"This is your big, terrifying pigeon?!"

"You saw it!" he tried to explain. "They were monsters!"

But it was no use. They weren't listening to him anymore. The backup officers dragged the Bird Poop Cop out of the pump station.

Pete airlifted us to safety a few blocks away. We could keep a lookout for Mustang Sally from there. He'd have to surface sometime. Until then, we had some catching up to do.

I had to ask, "Have you been able to talk this whole time, and you were just messing with me?"

"I think I just needed time, you know?" Pete said. "I want to thank you for being so kind and patient . . . and cleaning up after my *unfortunate* accidents."

"Yeah, that wasn't great, man. I laid down newspapers."

"And I read them all!"

I apologized to Pete. "I should have tried harder. A good leader doesn't just give orders, they listen."

"You really love your speeches, don't you?" Pete joked. "But it's okay. . . . Now we know what the East River Three want."

"We do?"

"Yeah, didn't you hear him? The Jersey Bight. I read about it. It's on display at the Natural History Museum. That's where Sally's going."

It all clicked into place.

I noticed the official-looking building across the street. At first glance, it looked like a library or a bank or something. But now I realized it was the Natural History Museum.

And it was conveniently located next door to the water pump station.

"Right next door . . . How does that help them?" I wondered out loud.

BOOOOM! Right on cue, I got my answer . . . as a geyser exploded through the pump station roof, shooting more water onto the streets.

The floods would rise. The city would sink. And the Pearl would be up for grabs.

Not on my watch.

CHAPTER 6
GOLDFIN

Fish rarely swim alone.

They need a school—a group of friends that have their back, no matter what. I thought of the East River Three that way, but there were some lines even they wouldn't cross at the beginning. Like helping me steal the Pearl.

That day I vowed to get it back, I wasn't just talking. I knew I'd do *anything* for it.

I just needed a certain kind of help my friends weren't ready to give me.

Criminal help. This led me to a human known as Bad Bernie. On the streets, he had a reputation for doing all sorts of *fishy* stuff, and I don't mean swimming. I mean robbery. If anyone could help us heist the Pearl, it'd be him.

Some time ago, I paid him a visit at an old pool hall on the edge of town. I told him my story—about changing under the water and getting exiled from my home. He listened politely. But when I mentioned the Pearl, he became *very* interested in what I had to say.

"The pearl you're talking about, it's worth millions," Bad Bernie said. "You bring it to me, and I'll make you the King of the Seas."

He paused to take a bite of his lunch. It was a plate of multicolored rolls he called "sushi." He could call it by whatever name he wanted, but I knew a fish when I saw one. And Bad Bernie was eating dead fish right in front of me. He didn't even bother to cook it first.

"Here's the thing," Bad Bernie continued, "last time I dealt with mutants, it didn't go so good. I gotta know I can trust you."

He slid the plate toward me.

"I can give you everything you want," he assured me. "All you gotta do is eat the sushi."

I picked up a piece, and I could feel my stomach turn. Sharks ate fish, I didn't. My entire life, all I'd eaten were plants and the occasional mosquito.

I knew humans ate my kind, but I never imagined I would, too. Bad Bernie eyeballed me, waiting for me to take a bite.

So that's what I did. I gulped the tuna down. There was no going back.

"Whoa! I honestly can't believe you did that!" Bad Bernie said, impressed.

I couldn't believe it either. But it's like I said, I'd have done anything to get the Pearl back.

Anything.

It was truly a *perfect storm*!

We'd all done our parts. Lee the Eel had burrowed her way through the sewers, cracking up the surface and blocking all the tunnels. Mustang Sally had sabotaged the city's pumps, guaranteeing the waters would stay on the rise. And me? I made sure everything went according to plan.

And now I would get to do what I'd set out to do that fateful day under the pier.

I'd get to be reunited with the Pearl.

All I had to do was wait for the tide to come in.

WHOOOOSH! A wave of water crashed through the Natural History Museum. It rushed out from the pumps and flowed through the halls, down the stairs, and even shot up from the toilets.

Which was how I arrived. I swam up through a toilet... just as a human was about to answer the call of nature.

"Some bad timing you got!" I teased.

BOOOM! Lee the Eel burst through the toilet next, sending the human flying out of the bathroom stall with his pants still around his ankles.

Mustang Sally soon joined us, crashing her way through the wall.

The water continued to pool up all around us, making it feel like old times. Like we were back home. The East River Three were swimming together again!

I finally got to see parts of the ocean I'd only dreamed of. Coral reefs and gigantic clams. I had to hand it to the museum workers—everything in this place almost looked real. *Almost.*

We swam into a so-called ocean exhibit, careful to stay under the laser lights and trip wires that covered the room wall-to-wall. From under the water, I could spot many watchful eyes. Bad Bernie told me these were called "security cameras."

Mustang Sally surfaced quickly and took care of those with a few barnacles from her slingshot.

No one was watching us now.

I glided toward a pedestal guarded by lasers in the center of the exhibit. There, propped up under the lights, glowing like a beacon in the dark was . . . the Pearl.

It would soon be mine. I moved forward, as did Lee the Eel—until a familiar face made her stand up in shock. "Teddy! What did they do to you?"

She was talking to a fake squid. And standing right in the light.

This tripped the alarm, and a loud, booming sound suddenly filled the air. More lasers activated, surrounding the Pearl. Lights so narrow, not even I could parkour through them.

I'd have to find another way in.

POOOOM! I fired a grappling hook and lowered myself into position. Then I snagged the Pearl and prepared to lift myself out. . . .

Only I noticed the hook that was holding me was about to give way. There was too much weight on it. I was about to drop!

PLINK! The hook came loose, and I plummeted with the Pearl—

Until something large and flat swooped in for me like a safety net. Only this was no net; it was a clamshell. A museum piece that Lee the Eel threw like a disc to catch me at the last second. And to carry me away from the lasers.

It worked!

I sat up, floating safely on top of the water . . . with the Pearl.

The others swam up, marveling at it. It was an emotional sight for them.

"I forgot how beautiful it is," Lee the Eel said.

"We can finally go home," Mustang Sally said, relieved.

"Question: How are we going to get it out?"

The sound of splashing got our attention. Human guards were wading through the water in the next room, making their way toward us.

We needed to fake them out.

What better way to do that than by faking it ourselves?

We quickly imitated the other museum pieces floating nearby. Plastic whales, sharks, and seals, frozen forever with their eyes open, perfectly still.

We each took a mannequin pose and let the floodwater carry us right past the human guards. They thought we were part of the exhibit!

I even heard one of them say, "They really are so lifelike!"

If only he knew.

DONATELLO

Our way back to the lair was blocked, and we were running out of time.

Literally. I was watching the seconds tick away on a digital timer that was attached to a roll of dynamite sticking out of the rubble. Raph had made the discovery and wasn't taking it well.

"Wanna tell me what I'm looking at here?" he said, agitated. "Because it looks like a whole bunch of dynamite ready to explode. But it can't be, right? Tell me this thing's not gonna explode."

"It's going to explode," I said.

"God, you're the worst, Donnie."

"What do you want me to do . . . lie?"

Wingnut stepped forward to take a look for herself. "Who would want to blow up the sewers?"

"It's these East River Three guys," Raph speculated. "There's a goldfish, a seahorse, and some kind of snake. According to their map, they're gonna rob the Natural History Museum. All this . . . it's like a distraction or something."

Not a bad plan . . . flooding the sewers and the city during a storm. The cops would be too busy to notice a robbery.

I went in for a closer look at the explosive device. I'd already wrestled gators and evaded monsters that night. I was happy to see something with wires and circuits that I could easily take apart.

"Maybe I can disarm it, but it'll take time," I told Raph, hoping it would be enough to calm him down. But he was way too fired up.

"We don't have time! We gotta get to the museum and stop those mutants!" he said.

"Dad's down here, our home is down here," I reminded him. "If the sewer walls go down—"

Scumbug suddenly spoke up. Well, *squeaked* up in vermin.

"What'd she say?" I asked.

Wingnut translated: "She said we'll deal with the explosives. You two go after the river mutants."

I looked at Raph. That sounded like a strategy we could all agree on.

"We've got this," Wingnut said heroically.

Then, away from the other Mutanimals, she whispered, "Just, ummm . . . Could you quickly teach me how to disarm this thing? You know, the broad strokes, the basics."

I didn't have time for a bomb tutorial! I barely had a second to freak out.

LEONARDO

There, on the steps of the Natural History Museum, it felt like I was up against impossible odds: a crew of mutant thieves and the storm of the century. And I had to try to stop it all and save the city by myself. A ninja alone.

Well, Pete was also there. I let him in on my game plan. "We go in there, full ninja stealth mode. I need to know I can count on you."

Pete just stared at me, blinking. "Actually, I'm still learning how to count. So you start with one ... it's crazy that two follows one. You will never guess what's next!"

"I'm gonna die," I sighed, hopeless.

Until I heard a voice across the street yell, "LEO!" Followed by the sound of a frog croaking.

It was Mikey! And Genghis!

I could have done a cartwheel I was so happy to see them. "Mikey! Genghis! What are you doing here?"

"We went to get snacks and got attacked by a giant mutant eel. We think she's headed this way," Mikey said.

Okay, I thought. *Two Turtles, one Mutanimal, and one Pete. I'm starting to like our chances. . . .*

Just as I was about to rerun the game plan with them, more reinforcements arrived from the sewers!

It was Donnie! And Raph!

We had all weathered the storm and were back together for a full-on Teenage Mutant Ninja Turtle reunion!

"You're all here! This is amazing!" I cheered.

"Uhhh, hey . . . ," Raph said, pointing at the pump station. "What's with that building? It's like a giant exploding water balloon over there."

I explained what had happened with Mustang Sally, and how it was all a big distraction from the real crime happening next door in the museum . . . all thanks to the East River Three.

"They're over there," Pete said, calmly pointing them out.

We turned, seeing them emerge from the museum doors—the heist was complete. Mustang Sally carried the Pearl over his shoulder.

Mikey leaned on me. "So . . . Pete talks now?!"

"Shhh!" I shushed him. We'd catch up later. Now was the time to approach with ninja stealth and surprise the bad guys on the steps! We flipped into action!

The goldfish came forward—he must have been the leader. "If you know what's good for you, you'll stay out of our way."

I tried to reason with them, but Raph clearly wanted to throw down. "Actually, we have no idea what's good for us! So let's—"

"*Not* start a fight," I said, finishing his sentence

before he could make things any more tense. "We're just talking. We're all being super reasonable."

Mikey also tried to keep the peace. "Yeah, these guys aren't our enemies!"

Donnie disagreed. "Uhhh, they're trying to blow up the seawall and flood the entire city."

Some of us were hearing this for the first time . . . including Sally and his eel friend! They were clearly shocked by this news.

"We're doing *what*?!" they cried.

The goldfish quickly changed the subject. "They're lying! They just want the Pearl for themselves! ATTACK!"

Raph got his wish.

The East River Three came straight at us with everything they had. We blocked their hits as best we could, but they were fierce fighters. With our ninja agility, we managed to snatch the Pearl from them and play keep-away with it, lobbing it over their heads. . . .

But this didn't last long.

Neither did we!

For a tiny guy, the goldfish was powerful. I saw him topple Raph and stomp Mikey out like a villain three times his size! I saw Sally knock Genghis out with one shell from his slingshot. The eel was there to finish us all off with a bang. . . .

Actually, a *spark*.

She unleashed a few thousand volts from her tail, electrifying the floodwaters that we were all standing in! In a flash, we were shell-shocked!

As I lay there, twitching, the whole world went black.

The last thing I heard wasn't my brothers crying out in pain, but another noise.

A sort of . . . *splat*.

PIGEON PETE

My friends were in trouble.

So I did what pigeons do best. I pooped.

A *lot*.

I hope I helped!

MICHELANGELO

By some miracle, the electricity stopped.

When I came to, I saw Lee the Eel running around,

covered from head to tail in a strange-looking splat of white-and-brown slime.

Bird poop.

Pete must have hovered during the fight and launched a poop bomb the size of Brooklyn right on top of her head. It was glorious . . . and so, so unsanitary!

I got to my feet and hugged Pete. "Did you just poop to save our lives? I'm so proud!"

"Well, you know, I don't have a weapon like you gentlemen," Pete said. "So I had to *make doo,* so to speak."

And he had jokes! My guy!

WHAM! I heard something hit hard. It was Lee's tail. It accidentally smacked right into a museum column, cracking it right down the middle.

I didn't know much about old buildings, but I knew that wasn't good!

I saw pieces of the roof starting to fall down.

I quickly helped my bros and Genghis up, and then I saw the seahorse mutant trying to do the same. He wanted to help Lee the Eel off the steps, away from the crumbling debris. He even ditched the Pearl to do this!

I knew what had to be done. "We gotta help them!"

"Guys! The goldfish!" Raph said, motioning for us to look the other way.

The goldfish was dragging the Pearl away from the scene, abandoning the other river mutants. I didn't think goldfish were that cold-blooded, but turned out, this one was!

He stopped to look back at us . . . and left us with a going-away gift.

The little guy shot out these huge, sharp blades from his fins. They sliced through the air over our heads, piercing the other columns!

The ground underneath us shook! Rocks and debris rained down!

The museum was collapsing on top of us!

RAPHAEL

I didn't know which was worse: the clouds in the sky or the giant cloud that landed on top of us, fogging everything up.

Dust.

The front of the museum had crumbled and kicked up a dust cloud that made it hard to see anything past the flood. While I could hear the others searching for the river mutants in the wreckage, I kept my eyes peeled . . . for the fish. There was no sign of him.

"Where's the Pearl?" Leo asked.

"He must have taken off with it," I said.

"If he gets away with the Pearl, everyone's gonna blame mutants. We have to—"

"KICK THAT FISH'S BUTT," I said, cutting him off. "I'm with you, but Mikey's gonna look at me with those sad eyes if we don't help them."

I let out a long huff. I guess we were going to let the bad guy get away for a change.

"No," someone piped up, like the voice of reason.

To my surprise, it was featherhead. I mean, *Pete.*

"You guys go after Goldfin. He said he was going to the pier. Genghis and I will free the river mutants," Pete suggested.

And you know what? I actually agreed with the bird guy for once!

Right on cue, there was Mikey with his sad eyes. "I made him!" he bragged, squeezing Pete.

It was a nice moment—which meant Leo was about to ruin it with his cool-guy deep voice.

"All right, guys, let's finish this," he said, in a low growl. "Together."

We all rightfully mocked him for it!

"Every time with this!"

It was classic.

GOLDFIN

As promised, I delivered the Pearl to Bad Bernie and his goons.

I dragged it down the pier and right up to the old man's yacht. Part of me wished the other members of the East River Three were here for this, but that wasn't the deal I'd made.

Besides, they would never have gone through with it if they had known. They were still hung up on making this thing a home again. I knew those days were long gone. I didn't let it get to me—as I've heard it said, *There are plenty of other fish in the sea.*

And sometimes those fish were human criminals with lots of treasure to throw around.

"You and I are going to be very rich men," Bad Bernie said, before choosing his words more carefully. "Mutants . . . whatever."

Suddenly something interrupted our meeting. I could hear a commotion happening on the deck. Bad Bernie's goons had spotted stowaways onboard. . . .

Rats.

They swarmed the humans and caused a panic. Even Bad Bernie seemed frightened and confused about where they were coming from.

But I knew.

I looked down the pier and saw him: the Rat King.

APRIL

The look on Goldfin's face was priceless.

Splinter and I rolled up to the pier with every rat in New York City backing us up. They had Bad Bernie's yacht covered; it looked like a hairy boat!

"You think you can threaten my family?" Splinter shouted to him. "Think again."

"Yeah, that's what you *get,* fish!" I added, feeling like the toughest high school reporter in the game.

I wasn't just witnessing the news—I was part of it! And it felt *amazing*.

WINGNUT

We hadn't made too much progress with the bomb since Donnie left. In fact, we hadn't made any progress. We just watched the timer tick down to 7:43 . . .

7:42 . . .

7:41 . . .

"Do something!" Leatherhead said anxiously. "We just need a big hole to throw these things down!"

What was she talking about? The entire sewer system was one big hole, and that hadn't helped us defuse this situation!

Scumbug started her squeaking again. Like that was gonna help us. I sighed. "Nobody knows what you're—"

But I understood her this time. She was pointing at Ray Fillet, who was now holding a bag of some kind. The bag was beeping.

I looked back at the rubble, shocked to see the dynamite missing.

Ray had taken the bomb and was running away with it, back down the tunnels. His voice echoed in the darkness. "RAY FILLEEEEEETTTTT!"

"Ray!" I cried. "Come back!"

LEONARDO

We hustled to the pier to catch Goldfin, who was already aboard Bad Bernie's yacht. With hundreds . . . no, thousands . . . of rats! I wondered what the little guys were doing here, but they seemed to be on our side, taking out Bad Bernie's boys for us.

That left us to finish Goldfin. Four against one. That was what I'd call *smooth sailing.*

"We just want the Pearl," I said.

"No one has to get hurt," Mikey added.

Goldfin had other ideas. He charged us with incredible speed, zipping through the air, right past our punches and kicks. It was like trying to attack a blur—I aimed, threw my fist, and accidentally wound up clocking Raph.

Weapons were no match for his quickness either. Donnie swung his bo staff wildly and whacked Mikey upside the head by mistake!

The worst part: he was winning, and he wasn't even tired yet. He fired fin blades at us, making us all duck and cover. Lying down on the deck made us easy targets for his barrage of head kicks and stomps.

Goldfin had us beat. He launched himself through the air, aiming to finish us off . . . when an even quicker hand caught him in midair.

It was another rat. *The biggest one of them all.*
Dad.

In an unbelievable display of ninja dominance, Dad easily overpowered Goldfin. With a simple flick of his wrist, he flung the fish against the ship's wheel, knocking him for a loop.

"This is no longer about home for you, is it, Goldfin?" Dad asked, like he'd dealt with him before.

"You think I was actually gonna drop that Pearl back in the river? Those fish down there rejected us!" Goldfin said with disgust. "I'm gonna use that Pearl to live like a king! Like Bad Bernie!"

I looked around to see if the others were as stunned by his lies as I was.

Yep, they were. Especially the new faces I saw climbing aboard: Pigeon Pete, Genghis, Mustang Sally, and Lee the Eel.

"You betrayed us," Mustang Sally said, looking truly hurt.

"That's cold," Lee said.

Goldfin was shocked to see the other river mutants alive. His voice got shaky. "Sally . . . Lee . . . wait. We can split the Pearl; we can have anything we want!"

The river mutants couldn't be bribed so easily. This wasn't about wealth for them, and they had bought enough of Goldfin's lies.

"We just wanted to be with you," Lee said.

Mustang Sally agreed. "That's what home means . . . being with the people you care about."

Goldfin had no more allies left—he was outnumbered, and he knew it. We made our move to capture him . . .

. . . when he suddenly made a run for it.

Seriously! Goldfin ran circles around us at, like, supersonic speed, wrapping us in one of the heavy ropes from the yacht as he went.

We were all tied up! Us bros, Dad, the Mutanimals, and the river mutants.

Goldfin didn't think twice about throwing us all overboard.

We hit the water with a *SPLASH!*

I climbed out of the river with everyone else and back onto the pier—just in time to watch Bad Bernie's yacht sail into the sunset.

Goldfin was getting away.

"He's got the Pearl!" Mikey said.

I wanted to go after him so bad—we all did. But how could we follow? We'd need a speedboat, or a rocket pack, or something that could glide on water.

Raph rubbed his eyes. "Ray?"

It was like the ocean answered him. A second later, we all heard . . .

"RAY FILLET!"

And there he was—the fastest mutant on water, with the sweetest singing voice. He swam toward us, carrying something in his fins. *Was that a duffel bag?*

"What's he holding?" Mikey asked.

Donnie cringed. "Yeahhhh . . . I didn't tell you guys about the dynamite, did I?"

"DYNAMITE?!" I shouted.

"You can use the explosives to stop the boat!" Pigeon Pete suggested. *That bird-pooping genius!*

"Great idea, Pete!" I said. "Let's do this!"

Ray Fillet tossed us the explosives, and we were off, in hot pursuit! There we were, four Turtles sprinting into the wind, racing toward the end of the pier like our lives depended on it.

In the world's most dangerous game of Hot Potato, we passed the bomb bag around, trying to toss it to whoever was out in front—whoever had the best shot of blowing the bad guys out of the water.

I peeked at the timer.

3 . . .

Donnie lobbed the dynamite up to Raph. . . .

2 . . .

Raph flung it my way as the end of the pier came up fast and the bow got closer and closer. . . .

1 . . .

I caught the bag and spiked it through the air in one swift motion.

It flew . . . beeping . . .

Right into the yacht—*KABOOOOM!*

The explosion was massive, scary, and without a doubt one of the coolest things I'd ever seen in my entire life.

SPLINTER

In the end, Goldfin's plan failed. The rains finally stopped. And the sun shone once again. . . .

On all of us.

But not on the Pearl.

No, not because it was destroyed in the blast. Quite the opposite! The explosion launched the curious object back into the water, where it belonged. I like to imagine new little goldfish and seahorses and eels swimming around it.

The Natural History Museum got a pearl back, too. Not the real one, but a brand-new one that Pigeon Pete may have helped create . . . in his own special, poopy way. How else were we going to provide a big ball of white stuff to take the Pearl's place? Trust me, the humans will be none the wiser!

Everyone else lived happily ever after. Like Lee and Sally, who now live together on a nice houseboat. Sally's babies are due any day now.

As for me and the Turtles and the Mutanimals, we saved the city . . . and each other . . . together.

And now we're back where we belong, too.

At home.

APRIL

So there you have it.

Raph helped it seem like Splinter was speaking and not squeaking, finally, but . . . this?! This was *unbelievable*!

This was supposed to be my interview about the storm. It sounded like something from a TV show.

Raph paused the new footage, eager to hear what I thought about his version of the story. "Pretty good, right? It had action, monsters, fighting . . . that's what people want!"

He wasn't wrong, but, c'mon! Who would ever believe such a tale?